A DEADLY COVER

COVER

A.S. MOST

Visit our website at www.StillwaterPress.com for more information.

First Stillwater River Publications Edition

ISBN-13: 978-1-952-52199-7
1 2 3 4 5 6 7 8 9

Library of Congress Control Number 2020909022

Written by A.S. Most
Cover design by Emma St. Jean

Published by Stillwater River Publications, Pawtucket, RI, USA.

Publisher's Cataloging-In-Publication Data
(Prepared by The Donohue Group, Inc.)

Names: Most, A. S., author.
Title: A deadly cover / A.S. Most.
Description: First Stillwater River Publications edition. | Pawtucket, RI, USA : Stillwater River Publications, [2020]
Identifiers: ISBN 9781952521997
Subjects: LCSH: Pharmaceutical industry--Corrupt practices--Fiction. | Drug traffic--Fiction. | Poisons--Fiction. | Graduate students--Fiction. | Neurologists--Fiction. | LCGFT: Detective and mystery fiction.
Classification: LCC PS3613.O7885 D43 2020 | DDC 813/.6--dc23

BOOK ONE

CHAPTER ONE

The nighttime late summer weather was perfect for an outdoor event and the rooftop venue lent the party a mildly exotic flavor. The roof was crowded so the party had expanded onto the adjacent building's roof. A four foot wide gangway with side rails served as the bridge joining the two buildings. The gap between them was only three feet, but that was enough to inspire caution in those venturing across the 'bridge.'

In this section of the East Village, five and six story tenements had survived the redevelopment mania that was populating Manhattan with giant steel and glass structures. It was only a matter of time before the East Village succumbed to the developer's juggernaut.

Beer, wine, and various odd brands of vodka were in good supply. The host and hostess lived in the building and were also the owners. Anyone with an invitation, and there were many, who had the energy to climb five flights of stairs in this walkup, was welcome.

Leslie Nugent, with sleeves rolled up, was fishing in the cooler's ice bath for a bottle of beer she could recognize. She was the guest of invitee Tony Mason, a friend and fellow reporter at *The Times*. Tony lived in the neighborhood and was a bowling teammate of the host, ergo his invitation.

Leslie, at thirty-four, drew male eyes wherever she went. Men saw a slim, athletic figure with straight, light brown, shoulder length hair framing a face with bright eyes, generous lips, and a mouth slightly turned up at the corners.

She clutched her dripping bottle of beer by its neck and wandered alone through the crowd. The roof was dimly lit by oil lanterns suspended from a wire that ran the perimeter of both rooftops.

A guy nearby called out to her, "Hey, lonely woman, didn't I see you come in with Tony?"

She turned toward him and answered, "You did, Hawkeye. Do you know Tony?"

"I sure do. We're bowling teammates. Can't be any more intimate than that. I'm Manny Rufalo."

"Nice to meet you, Manny. Do you perchance have a church key to open this warming bottle of beer?"

"My pocket knife serves that purpose. Gimme the bottle and you're on your way to quenching your thirst."

Leslie handed him the bottle and he produced an opener on a pocket knife. He handed the open bottle back to her and she took a long swig.

Manny was just her height at five foot seven. He was a somewhat dark-skinned, muscular guy with curly black hair and dark eyes. A thick black moustache completed the picture of a Mediterranean male. The horizontal striped polo shirt gave him the appearance of a gondolier. She smiled to herself as she made this quick assessment.

"Hey, Leslie, I finally found you," remarked Tony. "Better be careful around this guy. Manny's been trying to organize a woman's bowling team and only seems to approach the most attractive women. It's his come-on opener. So far there are no recruits."

"I haven't received an offer, Tony. So that must say something about me."

"Okay, you guys. Enough ragging on my bowling start-up. I'm gonna move on to more fertile fields. Nice to meet you, Miss Who-Never-Gave-Me-Her-Name."

"I'm sorry, Manny. I'm Leslie Nugent. And I am pleased to meet you, even if I didn't meet your bowling league standard."

Manny melted into the crowd.

"Are you friendly with Manny, Tony? He doesn't seem your type. What does he do?"

"Good question, Leslie. I'm not sure, but I think he's connected to pharmaceuticals. Some of the guys think he's involved in the dark side of the drug business. I just don't know."

Leslie and Tony were silent for a moment as they thought about Manny.

"See that fellow over there with a cane, Leslie? That's Steve Meyerson. He was on our team. Unfortunately, he's developed a problem walking and has had to give up bowling. He was our best roller a year ago. I've heard that Steve is also a long-time drug user. I think Manny is his supplier. No proof, just a suspicion."

The two of them crossed the "bridge" to the adjacent roof where more party was ongoing. Leslie recognized a woman she knew from work, a copy editor, and walked over to join her.

"Hi, Evelyn. Didn't expect to meet anyone here that I knew."

"Hi, Leslie. Nice to see you. Let me introduce you to some friends. This is Ann-Marie Jordan, a friend from way back, and this is Gary Ellis, her husband. Gary is a dancer with the City Center Ballet Company."

"Nice to meet you folks. I'm here with Tony Mason, Evelyn. You probably know Tony from the paper."

"Of course I do, Leslie. Let me take you over to the bar so you can grab another brew to replace that empty you're carrying around. Excuse us for a minute, guys."

They walked across the roof to an area that acted as a self-serve bar.

"I'm sorry I pulled you away so abruptly, Leslie. I wanted to clue you in to the problem facing the couple I was with when you joined us. It might avoid some embarrassment. Gary is a user who's trying to get clean. Unfortunately, he's developed unpredictable mood swings which may be related to drugs. He may also be having mood problems because he was just put on indefinite leave by the dance company. His dancing days may be over since he's lost some feeling in his legs. I just wanted you to be aware of the difficulty that couple is dealing with, in case Gary should act up. Now, get yourself a drink and we can go back to join them."

Eventually the evening wound down and Leslie and Tony left the scene. They parted with a friendly kiss on the cheek.

Later that evening Leslie sat in her bed planning to read herself into a drowsy state, but the evening had set her mind working, wide-awake. Her nose for a story was on alert. Two youngish guys on drugs with leg problems. Was there a connection? She wondered if it was worth pursuing. For the time being she'd file it away for future consideration.

CHAPTER TWO

The trees lining the driveway were in full flower on a beautiful summer morning. Larry Crandall took it all in and felt his mood lifted up by the serenity of the setting. He pulled into his reserved parking space and sat a minute while he reflected on the peaceful scene.

A knock on his car window broke his train of thought. Mitch Trent, his partner in Sampson Industries, was smiling and motioning to walk with him into the factory office suite. Larry got out of the car, grabbed his briefcase from the back seat, greeted Mitch, and the two of them walked to the building.

Mitch had a generous office befitting the COO and junior partner in the company. The senior partner and company president, Larry Crandall, had his office directly opposite Mitch's. No one else was in at this early hour, so Mitch got coffee for each of them from the staff room Keurig. He joined Larry in the latter's office and they began a discussion of needed plant improvements. The subject was one they'd been working over for several weeks. Sampson's plant was nearly twenty years old and needed a number of updates, particularly ventilation in the chemical preparation area.

The chemical plant that was Sampson Industries was situated in a wooded area in Yonkers, New York, less than half an hour's drive from Manhattan. The area, touted as an industrial park, was home to several light industry companies.

Larry and Mitch were both in their mid-fifties. Larry didn't share Mitch's taste for risk and penchant for high living. Whereas Larry and Elaine Crandall were a clean-living, traditional couple with two career-oriented children, Mitch and Brenda Trent were each working on a second marriage after divorces and their only children were the offspring of Mitch and his ex-wife. He had substantial alimony payments to make along with college expenses and a current wife with expensive taste.

Sampson Industries ran in the black, but it hadn't created the kind of profit margin that would meet the expectations of its two senior executives. For Larry a smooth road with a reasonable income was sufficient. For Mitch there had to be more. He was skating on thin ice.

Larry had recently brokered an arrangement with a smaller chemical company, York Chemical, which was an undocumented partnership. Mitch knew very little about the background of that arrangement. Larry had negotiated it personally and didn't include Mitch in any discussions. The two companies continued as independent businesses. The only change was that some of the products Sampson produced for York were granted a high priority and were manufactured under very tight security. Sampson held contracts for all the work done in their plant, including the work for York.

Sampson's new association held out the promise of increased profits. That would please both Larry and Mitch, but particularly Mitch. The revenue from York explained why the balance sheet had improved so much.

Mitch accepted the new product lines for York as business as usual and credited Larry with good rainmaker skills. Larry's personal impetus in forging the new company arrangement would remain secret for the time being.

CHAPTER THREE

L arry Crandall looked older than his fifty-five years. His thin face was heavily lined and his long hair was mostly grey. Clean-shaven, he was an average looking guy at just under six feet with a lean body. In a worn, brown corduroy sport coat with leather elbow patches, smoking a pipe, he had the appearance of a small town college professor.

He worried that he'd gone about as far as his training and experience were going to take him. His career had been unblemished by scandal or underhanded dealings. He needed something to prove to himself that his creative juices hadn't dried up. Something that would convince him that he still had good years ahead. He did this by using his chemical knowhow in a way that brought him personal satisfaction. No one else need know. *He* would know and that would be enough.

He'd incubated a plan for several years and now it was ready for implementation. He identified a chemical that was a distant cousin to crystal methamphetamine, a street drug with serious side effects. It was less potent and far more difficult to manufacture. It had been set aside by drug sellers in favor of the more toxic "real thing."

Larry studied the chemical structure and saw a way, with slight modifications, to incorporate it into a harmless chemical, the "mother chemical," from which it could later be recovered. Larry had it in his mind to do something unique. Sampson was legitimate, making chemical products for other companies to package and sell or add to some product they were ready to bring to market. Larry's ploy would be to produce "mother chemicals" that could be modified by a secondary company to yield illegal drugs while leaving behind a benign product for legitimate use. The discarded remains of the "mother chemical" in this case would serve as an innocent additive in a wood preservative marketed under the York name. This would serve as cover for the darker chemical manipulation.

Mitch was unsuspecting at the beginning.

Larry knew of Oscar Gleason and saw his company, York Chemical, as the ideal mate for Sampson. He knew Gleason's background involved illegal drug dealing but thought they could work together, albeit at a distance. He met Gleason privately and pitched the idea to him. It was exactly the type of business Gleason was interested in. York Chemical was struggling and needed to make a bold move. Larry and Oscar came to a handshake agreement.

York Chemical delivered the very important outside services that completed Larry's plan. Gleason was his man dealing with the dark world of drugs while also serving as head of an otherwise legitimate company contracting with Sampson for product. The system certainly beat smuggling drugs across the border.

The wall between Oscar and Larry was formidable. Larry wanted to know very little. He didn't even want any part of the street profits. Sampson charged York Chemical a very high price to produce its product and that's where the company saw significant financial return on his creation. He wasn't after money. It gratified his need for personal achievement and confirmation that he still had creative ability. This completed Larry's magnum opus.

CHAPTER FOUR

Intermission at the revival of *Carousel* gave Elaine Crandall an opportunity to introduce herself to the man seated at her left. He appeared to be alone and sported no ring on his left hand. His loosely combed black hair was lightly flecked with grey. She guessed that he was about forty-five years old. He had the look, she thought, of an outdoorsman in big city clothes. She turned toward him in her seat and, offering her best smile, asked how he was enjoying the show.

"So what do you think of the first act? Ever see it before?"

Before answering Bob gave her a quick once-over. He saw an attractive, middle-aged, sandy-haired woman with a friendly face. He'd bet she worked out regularly, too. He turned toward her in his seat and offered his best smile in response. She noted the perfect set of teeth.

"Well, I've seen the movie but find this live performance more emotional and appealing."

Elaine was quick to respond. "I couldn't agree more. I saw the original on Broadway when I was a little girl and this production is equally enchanting. I'm loving it."

"I was lucky to get this single seat. The theatre is sold out."

"Let me introduce myself. I'm Elaine Crandall and the quiet guy on my right is my husband, Larry." Larry leaned across his wife and the two men shook hands.

"Bob Hillman's my name. Nice to meet the two of you." Bob appeared interested in continuing the conversation so Elaine quickly shifted into a personal line of inquiry.

"Are you a New Yorker, Bob, or from out of town?"

"That's not easy to answer, Elaine. My home is in San Francisco but I'm living temporarily for this year in New York. I've only been here two weeks, but I like the feel of the city and find it not unlike San Francisco."

"We live in Scarsdale but have a pied-a-terre here in Manhattan that we use when we're in the city." Elaine continued digging in a friendly manner. "Single ticket. No wedding ring. Clues say you're living here alone."

He smiled broadly and Elaine was warmed by the way his charming manner deflected her intrusive questioning.

"Right on. I temporarily left my good life on the West Coast and am beginning to settle in here. If everyone's as friendly as you, it won't be long before it'll feel like home."

"Well, before the intermission is over, tell me what you do."

"I'm a businessman and I'm looking to expand my west coast business here in the New York area. What's my business? It's energy development, sale and innovation. Things like natural gas, oil, solar, and wind power."

Elaine was relentless. She reached into her small evening purse.

"Okay. You passed the test. Here's a picture and a phone number. The woman is my daughter, Denise. She'd be well worth a call and a lunch. Trust me. It would be a small step toward settling in here in New York."

The house lights dimmed.

"It looks like intermission is over. Nice meeting you, Bob."

They parted with a handshake after the show was over. As he started slowly walking toward his apartment, he took the picture she had given him out of his jacket pocket. Her daughter was an appealing blond woman, dressed for running. She had an athletic build and her mother's engaging smile. Probably worth a call.

Walking up Eighth Avenue he got caught up in a recurring memory that wouldn't go away. He hadn't had a serious woman friend in over two years. His last companion had deserted him when he made it apparent that they had no permanent future to look forward to. She quickly found a mate whom she could make a life with and had done just that.

He couldn't understand what was keeping him from forming a serious and then permanent attachment. Living a solitary life wasn't particularly appealing, but he didn't seem able to jump into the social stream and find a mate. He conjured up a variety of personal events in his life, but they didn't seem to explain what he considered a failing on his part. As usual he was able to brush aside this unpleasant thought and get on with his busy life.

CHAPTER FIVE

Marjorie Cameron, a fortyish brunette with a playful smile and piercing green eyes, was the Human Resources officer for Sampson Industries. Sitting at her desk she was puzzled by the latest month's employment report. Just as in the previous two months, absenteeism was down significantly. The previous months had been considered an anomaly and were given little attention. Now, three months with the same employment data required an explanation. The Executive Committee would expect a thoughtful analysis from her when she presented the statistical report at the next meeting. The data would be considered a big plus but that didn't obviate the need for an interpretation.

She dug into the data and quickly saw that the improved attendance was largely restricted to the chemical worker portion of the workforce.

Sampson Industries' major product output was chemicals used in the manufacture of commercial products sold largely in big-box hardware stores such as Home Depot and Lowes. What was there about chemical workers that made them so faithful to their jobs? A more detailed analysis was called for but would take some time. Perhaps her boss, Mitch Trent, would have some insight to offer.

CHAPTER SIX

Leslie's editor's office at *The Times* was a small cubicle with a dirty window facing out on the building next door. Clayton Garfield enjoyed his sessions with reporters. Bright young people with new story ideas were his lifeblood ever since he left the reporting life. A serious back problem had forced him to abandon chasing down stories. He still missed that, even after assuming an editor's job over five years ago.

Leslie, his newest reporter, was the one he most enjoyed meeting with. She had an irrepressible hunger for new storylines and could be counted on to respond with enthusiasm when offered one. You could say he lived vicariously through his reporters.

"Leslie, I have an unusual assignment for you. It's not exciting but you never can tell what an interview will turn up."

"Did you see my shoulders sag, Clay? Of course not. I'm game for whatever you dish out."

"Okay. There's a guy in town who's big in the energy game. He may be one of the good guys. He's here to speak with the mayor about putting together a plan for New York City to steadily move to reduced reliance on fossil fuels. I think he's a realist with a touch of idealism.

At least that's what my sources tell me. You can Google him and speak to people on the West Coast about him before you meet with him. Do anything you want to prepare for the interview. I've set it up and have all the particulars spelled out on this sheet of paper. The interview will take place after he meets with the mayor so that should broaden the scope of the story."

Garfield stopped here and gave Leslie a chance to respond.

"It's not my field of special expertise but I'll bone up on the subject and be ready for the interview. It'll be a change of pace for me to do a sit down interview. Thanks for the opportunity, Clay."

On that optimistic note, Leslie left his office. The afternoon was blending into evening and she had to decide whether to call one of her girlfriends to make dinner and evening plans. She was fortunate to have made good women friends, but male companionship was something she sorely missed. She'd always enjoyed a vigorous sex life, but since coming to New York that aspect of her life had failed to materialize. She wasn't one to settle for casual sex. A fellow had to please her in some other way that she found enjoyable beyond the basic animal need.

CHAPTER SEVEN

Marjorie handed Mitch a copy of the employment report. He gave it a cursory inspection and looked up at her from behind his Plexiglas desk.

"Okay, Marge, I give up. What's the big deal? We're doing something right and our employees are happy to work here."

Marjorie stifled her frustration. "It's not that simple, Mr. Trent. We need to understand what's happening with the chemical workers, not just pat ourselves on the back."

He put up his hands in mock self-defense, "Okay, Marge, let me look into this a bit. If I come up with anything interesting, we'll meet again and have a real discussion about it."

"Thanks, Mr. Trent. I just wanted to alert you to the finding and help us prepare for the executive committee meeting two weeks from yesterday."

"Enough with the 'Mr. Trent,' Marge. We've seen each other with a lot less clothing on than we're wearing right now. Which reminds me, aren't we meeting at The Bedford tomorrow afternoon for lunch?"

"Right. I'm looking forward to it. See you tomorrow, Mr. Trent." Marge ended this exchange with a smile."

"Okay, Marge."

She let herself out and Mitch turned his attention to the report.

CHAPTER EIGHT

Denise Crandall finished cleaning up her small apartment and turned her attention to the pile of books on her desk. In her final year of business school at Columbia she looked forward to graduation in the spring and the beginning of her real career. After graduating from Yale she had worked as a cub reporter at a newspaper in White Plains. She knew it was a way station but hadn't been sure what the next stop would be. After eight years she decided to get an MBA and then, coupling that with her reporter experience, market herself to a big paper as a business reporter. There had been several offers and she was now weighing her options. The last hurdle was writing a research paper on a business topic so she could earn the high honors her grades were pointing toward.

Her cellphone was ringing with a caller's name she couldn't identify. She decided to pick it up.

"Denise here. Who's Bob Hillman?"

"I'm looking at the picture your mother gave me at the theatre a few nights ago. She's a charmer and a good saleslady. She also gave me your number and told me you were worth a call and lunch. So, I'm doing the call and all that remains is the lunch."

"So, my mom's done it again. Picked up a stranger at the theatre and sicced him on her daughter. Her thirty-two-year-old daughter, I might add."

"Okay, Denise. Where would you like to have lunch tomorrow?"

"Whoa. My mother may have hypnotized you but I don't easily sell out for a free lunch."

"Who said anything about free?"

"Well, now you're beginning to make some headway, Bob. Meet you at Barney Greengrass tomorrow at noon. I assume you're in Manhattan and can look up the address or just tell the Uber where you want to go."

"So far, so good, Denise. I'm six foot two and sometimes mistaken for Brad Pitt. I'll be wearing a blue shirt, khakis, and a navy V-neck. I'll know you from your picture unless it was taken ten years ago and you've added twenty pounds. Just kidding, of course. See you tomorrow."

CHAPTER NINE

Early evening and Mitch was still in the office. It had been a while since he had to do any serious data analysis. The report Marge had left with him was intriguing. No question. The chemical workers rarely missed a day of work. Okay, that's the obvious part. What was the explanation, if there was one? Other work groups in the plant didn't show similar changes. He began to dig a bit. The contract that group was working on called for brewing a liquid additive that was a component of a popular wood finish made by York. The contract was for a year and was now in its fourth month.

He spun his chair around and pulled a folder out of the file cabinet behind him. The folder was labeled 'plant improvements.' That area of the plant where the workers seemed to really enjoy mixing chemicals was due for a major improvement in its ventilation system. The old exhaust fan system in the area was scheduled for replacement this winter.

That would complete the upgrade project and keep Sampson in compliance with OSHA regulations.

So how did an old ventilation system figure in this puzzle, if it figured at all? If anything, he'd expect a less efficient ventilation system to sicken workers and hurt attendance. He needed to visit the area and see if he could identify any unusual aspects of the work or worksite that could contribute to the unexpected finding in the report.

CHAPTER TEN

It was a beautiful Indian summer day with a mixture of clouds and blue sky. Bob had no trouble finding Barney Greengrass and arrived a bit early. He also had no trouble recognizing Denise as she stepped out of a cab in front of the restaurant. He approached her slowly, not wanting to make her any more wary than she had been on the phone.

He saw an attractive young woman, taller than he anticipated, and dressed casually in black jeans and a pale blue cotton shirt. Her hair was shorter than in the picture and gave her an 'outdoorsy' look. The package was appealing. She saw a rugged, good looking guy with tousled black hair and an athletic looking body. He was an inch or two over six feet, half a foot taller than her five foot eight inches in flats. She liked a guy much taller than her.

"Hey, Denise Crandall. Nice to meet you in person." He held up his index finger. "Just remember I'm still under your mother's hypnotic trance, so don't snap your fingers and break the spell."

Denise laughed out loud. He took that as a good opening response. She couldn't be too tense and laugh so effortlessly.

"Hey yourself, Robert Hillman. I could eat a bear, so let's get a table and find out who we're each dining with."

With that they headed into the restaurant and were seated at a small table by the window. Denise was relaxed and relieved that her mother may actually have done well this time. At least judging by the opening salvos.

"Okay, Bob, what's your story? Let's get that out of the way so we can just talk friendly-like."

"My story is not simple, Ms. Crandall, so it may require a continuation into dinner tonight. Dutch treat, of course."

"If your story includes a spell in prison for some heinous crime, we can stop right here and enjoy a silent meal before parting company forever."

"I'm afraid it's just a bit convoluted, but not violent. Here's a somewhat abridged version. I grew up in Wyoming. My mother and father were killed in an auto accident when I was ten years old. My father's brother and wife were childless and adopted me. They were loving parents. My father and his brother had been partners in a mining business which had grown to be one of the largest privately owned mining companies in North America. As a teenager, I learned the business from the bottom up. I went away to Stanford and studied history but always had mining on the mind.

"After Stanford I was itchy for some excitement so I did two tours with the marines in Afghanistan. Two was more than enough. We can talk about it some other time, if there is another time." He smiled at her. "I came back to earth, studied mining at the University of Wyoming for three years, and received a master's degree in mining science. I then returned to the family business in Casper, Wyoming with many ideas on how to modernize the business.

"Two years later my uncle-father, a widower for a year, passed away and left me sole ownership of a very large mining company. Since then I've broadened the company's portfolio to include a large component of solar and wind power. Lastly, we also retrieve precious metals from the mine tailings through a patented process that makes up ten percent of our business. Is that enough or do you want to hear what the company does with its profits? Or what brings me to New York City? I told you it could run into dinner time."

"That's quite a story, Bob. As a future business reporter you can be sure I'd want to profile you. And, yes, I do want to hear what the company does with its profits. That's you though, isn't it? What do you do with your profits?"

"That's a rather long story too so I'll give you a very short version. I set up a not-for-profit foundation dedicated to helping disadvantaged youngsters make it to and through college. We focus on a largely rural area in northern California. The foundation is well-funded, yes, by me, and is beginning to have some success. I'll stop there."

"Did my mother know any of this when she handed you my picture and phone number?"

"No. But she does know that a business venture brought me to New York and a theatre seat at *Carousel*."

"Give me a minute while I try to absorb all that you've told me. Seems you could well afford to pay for my lunch, so withdrawing that free lunch offer suggests miserly instincts."

"As I recall it was you who intimated that there was an offer of free lunch and I denied having made any such offer."

"Well, let's settle that matter right now. Warren Buffett would pick up the check so I'd be pleased to let you spring for this meal. My mom will enjoy the story even more."

"My offer extends to anything on the menu, even that astonishingly expensive cold cut platter. Now, let me hear your story."

"OK. Here's the short, unabridged version. Middle class up-bringing, BA from Yale, eight years as a reporter in White Plains, New York and now finishing up an MBA at Columbia. No foundations, no mining empire, and no husband or children. You may want a pre-nup should we decide to marry."

"Let's order before we run into dinner and have to negotiate another bill."

Two hours later they left Barney Greengrass and agreed to have dinner the following night.

CHAPTER ELEVEN

Marjorie Cameron and Elaine Crandall belonged to the same gym in Yonkers and often had lunch together in the gym's spa after their workouts. Marjorie, being younger, was into weights while Elaine did moderate aerobics.

Lunch for each as usual consisted of a lot of lettuce with a smattering of additives: berries, fruits, cheese, grains, and some less well-known greens.

The younger woman often used Elaine as a confidant. Today she was venting her guilt about having an affair with a married man. Elaine, a good listener, could only offer the advice she would have given her daughter.

"Marge, I think you know where this winds up. You'll get hurt, his wife will get hurt, and he'll wonder why women are so unforgiving and lacking in understanding. The sooner it ends the better. Find a guy without a wedding ring."

"Yeah, I know you're right, Elaine, but somehow I seem to fall into this trap too easily."

"Marge, let's move on to some other topic. We've been over this ground before."

"Listen to this, Elaine. Sampson Industries is experiencing an unexplained reduction in absenteeism. It's no small matter. That's three months in a row. Even though it's good news I'm still looking for an explanation."

"That is interesting, Marge. Larry certainly hasn't said anything about it at home. I wonder if he even knows about it. He would mention it if he did, because that's about the excitement level of our dinnertime conversations."

"Well, it's recent news. I just brought it to Mitch's attention."

Elaine sat up straight in her chair and pointed a finger at her friend.

"That's serendipitous, Marge. Denise happens to be looking for a subject to use for her honors paper in business school. This might be a very good opportunity for her since she could have access to the company records and employees. Do you see any problem with me passing this information on to her?"

"None at all from my end. But try it out on your husband. If he okays it, you can just pass it on to Denise."

CHAPTER TWELVE

Drying her hair after a shower, Leslie stood in front of the bath-room mirror and had a moment of reflection on her recent love life. The break up with her recent beau in Washington had been painful for both parties. Leslie had lived through a tortuous and dangerous plot to cover up the president's illness. Her first-rate coverage had led to an invitation from the New York Times to join their top-flight news reporting staff.

She was deeply involved at the time with a doctor she'd met through her coverage of the story. They both saw the offer as a reporter's dream. It was an opportunity she couldn't say no to. It also meant a pause in their romance since his practice in North Carolina and her job in New York City put too much distance between them. They agreed to cool down the relationship and let time determine if it would be rekindled. They would stay in contact.

Now, living alone in a small one-bedroom apartment in Greenwich Village, Leslie found herself beginning to appreciate the excitement of life in New York City. At the paper she'd met several women reporters of a similar age who were always on the lookout for a drinking, eating, and partying companion—male preferably but always happy to have female companionship.

Tonight Leslie, Rosalind, and Bethany were standing at the crowded bar in Gladwell's Pub, a too-popular bar in the West Village. The noise was deafening and the smell was a mixture of beer, sweat, and perfume. The mood was joyful and that was what brought the crowds in. The tall, four dollar draft beers didn't hurt either.

Standing next to Leslie, vying for attention from one of the bartenders, was a six-foot male in a half zipped pullover sweater and jeans. The crowding was intense so he and Leslie were as close to intimate as strangers in public could get. He politely turned toward her and introduced himself.

"Chan Young, Ms. Whoever. If I was going to be crushed to death I couldn't imagine a more attractive person to be crushed along with."

"Leslie Nugent, Chan. I'll always remember your dying words."

Leslie saw a handsome Chinese-American guy with a playful smile, pearly teeth, and slightly greying, close-cut hair. His age was difficult to guess but she gauged him to be forty.

"Since we're locked in here together, Chan, let's get acquainted. I'm single, live in the Village, and only moved to New York six weeks ago from D.C. I'm a news reporter for *The Times*. Your turn."

"I'm single too, live in Brooklyn with two male roommates, and am a native New Yorker. I make my living as a cop. I'm a detective in the NYPD, Drug Division."

Leslie gave him a closer look now. He had a good sense of humor and made his living on the right side of the law. He was good looking too. Definitely better than average.

"I think the bartender is waiting for your order, Chan. Throw mine in as well and I'll buy the first round."

Chan placed the order. "Two draft Stellas. Thanks." The bartender moved on and soon returned with two ice cold beers.

Chan continued, "You said you'd pay for the first round. A bit presumptuous of you to assume we've become drinking buddies. Just because our bodies are molded into each other's doesn't mean we're really close in any other way."

"I didn't mean to frighten you, Chan."

"Well, us single guys are wary of being taken advantage of by aggressive females. Let me suggest we try dinner together tonight to find out if we really are meant to be 'beer buddies.' After these brews let's cut out and try to get into Sevilla where the paella is terrific."

"Sounds like a good plan, Chan. I like Sevilla. You're my first 'cop date.'"

"There you go again, Leslie. Jumping the gun. I didn't ask you out. I just suggested we get some dinner. I can see I have to be very guarded with you lest we find ourselves in bed together."

"Chan, you'll have to do more than share some paella with me before that'll happen. Now let's finish off these beers and see if we can tunnel our way out of here."

Growing up on Long Island as the youngest of three sisters, Leslie had evolved into a fearless, sometimes reckless woman. Her older sisters had provided their parents with six grandchildren, so Leslie felt no pressure to mate and procreate. Quite the opposite. She enjoyed a robust sex life with a string of eligible guys—some married but mostly single—and was fastidious about birth control measures. Her healthy good looks were naturally maintained with a good diet and regular exercise. She required a minimum of bottled beauty products.

Coupled with a solid career as a reporter, her good looks and natural sexuality made her very appealing to a long string of males who tried in vain to develop a long-term serious relationship. Inability to establish one or disinterest in a stable connection was the one bothersome element in her otherwise satisfying life situation.

CHAPTER THIRTEEN

The production area of interest in the recent report was quiet when Mitch made an early evening visit. The workday was over and all activity had ceased an hour ago. He reflected that it had been a long time since he actually paid a visit to the chemical section of the plant. On entry he was immediately aware of an odor in the air. The large exhaust fans in the ceiling were running hard but could not dispel the odor. He would have to visit the site during working hours to see if the odor was stronger during the hours when chemicals were being handled and vats were unsealed for sampling, testing, and adding ingredients.

Although the odor was strong it was not repellant. He recalled a number of instances in pharmacy school when chemical fumes had irritated the lining of his nose; he'd had to apply petroleum jelly to his nostrils. These fumes were not as burning. Not by a long shot.

He wandered through the very large room impressed by how clean it was. The people who worked there were obviously careful and respectful of their workplace.

He'd gained little insight into the matter of absenteeism, or rather lack thereof. A return visit during working hours would be his next step. A chat with some workers and another appraisal of the environment was called for.

CHAPTER FOURTEEN

An Uber met her New York Central train at the Scarsdale station and drove her to her parents' home. Denise last had dinner with her parents in their house, her old house, just after finishing her first year in business school. Before going in, she stopped to admire the street she grew up on. Large, old trees were just beginning to acquire their fall colors. That made this a very pleasing suburban scene. The houses were not the McMansions that were replacing older homes elsewhere in Scarsdale. She went in without ringing the bell.

Later, feasting on her own terrific veggie lasagna, Elaine impatiently delved into Denise's social life. Usually that waited until dessert, after they chatted about school, career, and other, relatively stress-free topics.

"Okay, Denise, let's hear about Mr. Hillman. You've only told me the barest bones about him. How many times have you gone out? What's he like? C'mon let loose."

"Well, here's the short version. We see each other quite often. Usually for dinner. And he pays. He's kind, gentle, and considerate. A perfect boy scout. He's bright without having to prove it and he's a good listener. He's handsome, as you know, and has a subtle sense of humor. In short, he's the best guy you ever sent my way. Hate to say it, Mom, but you really struck gold with this find."

"Wow, do you think he feels that way about you? Those traits you describe could be his description of my daughter. Anything else? Sounds like you're ready to set the date after half a dozen dinners."

"Oh, yes. Not that it matters, Mom, but he's very rich. And I do mean *very* rich. What does matter is that we seem so right for each other. Dad, you'd like him. In your fisherman lingo, he's a keeper."

"Do you think you can keep him?" was her dad's interested question.

"I'm going to do my damnedest unless I find some hidden flaw that could prove fatal."

"Denise, I hate to leave this subject that has me and your father panting, but there is a different subject I want to mention before you leave. I know you're looking for a topic for your honors paper. Marjorie mentioned to me that worker absenteeism at Sampson was way down for the third month in a row and that no one had a good explanation. I thought it might be a possible topic for an MBA student to research. Your dad could assure ready access to any documents. I thought I'd just throw this out to you. That's it."

"Sounds like a good lead. I'll give it serious thought. Thank Marge for me. And thanks for the terrific lasagna. Now how about that fresh fruit dessert I saw out in the kitchen?"

CHAPTER FIFTEEN

Bob was shaving and listening to NPR as he got ready for his breakfast meeting with George O'Reilly. They were meeting at the Yale Club at nine thirty for breakfast. George, an old friend from Stanford, and a Yale Law School graduate, was a senior aide to New York's mayor. Bob hoped George could offer some insight into the best approach to the mayor and whom he should meet to begin a discussion of ways to restructure the city's energy profile. It was an exploratory step, so he kept his expectations low.

On the other hand, his expectations rose with each meeting he had with Denise. After years of bachelorhood and many woman friends, he felt that this early relationship was different. They were a good fit. No, better than good. She raised his spirit and excited him in a way no woman had in recent years. He couldn't believe what good fortune that single ticket to *Carousel* had brought him.

Dinner tonight would be takeout from a very good Thai restaurant in the west eighties. Bob was looking forward to an evening of intimacy and a chance to find out if Denise was as eager as he was to experience sex in their relationship. There was no reason to hold back.

CHAPTER SIXTEEN

The chemical processing area was in full operation. Mitch entered without warning or fanfare. Most of the workers didn't recognize him but the foreman of the operation knew Mitch and came forward to greet him.

"Nice to see you, Mitch," was his casual greeting to the company COO. "Is there anything I can do for you?"

Mitch responded with an equally casual greeting. "Barry, I'm just hoping to get a firsthand feeling for each area in our enterprise. Like many execs, it's easy to become office-bound and never meet your employees or gain an understanding of the actual workings of the various units in this sprawling plant."

Mitch was aware of the chemical odor in this area. It was quite a bit stronger than what he experienced in his afterhours visit. He didn't plan to comment on it, however.

"Well, Barry, why don't you just walk me through the place and point out things you think I should be aware of. Remember, I did go to pharmacy school and have a general knowledge of chemistry."

"That'd be my pleasure. You can see we're in high gear, right on schedule to meet the production deadline in the current contract we're working under. We're making an additive to a product that sells nationally in large home supply stores."

They strolled slowly through a maze of stainless steel vats, stepping over thick lengths of flexible steel tubing. The hum of the exhaust fans was noticeable but Mitch made no comment about the prominent odor.

Barry opened the door to that subject. "I'm sure you can smell the chemical odor. You probably wonder why there's any odor at all since the vats and tubing are sealed. Well, chemicals have to be added and product sampled for quality. We're very careful when breaking seals but it's not a perfect system. There are also occasional mechanical problems resulting in open vats. The ventilation system is old and scheduled for repair. I'm sure that system's part of the problem contributing to the fumes. Given all that, our health record in this section has been excellent."

They continued wandering with Barry introducing him to workers along the way. Masks were hung on the wall but Mitch saw no one with a mask on. Barry indicated that the masks were worn at the site of any planned opening of the chemical stream.

Mitch looked up at the exhaust fans without appearing especially curious. He noted a fine coating of white powder on the inside of the fan frames. Again, he chose not to bring this up.

They wound down the tour and he warmly thanked Barry. He left several dozen lunch passes for the men and waved as he left through the self-sealing exit.

The fresh air was welcome. No question about it. The fumes were very potent. The powder on the fume hoods needed to be analyzed. He'd have to get a sample and bring it to an outside lab for analysis. Still, the problem was not illness or absence from work; it was unexplained lack of absence. This needed more thought.

CHAPTER SEVENTEEN

Thai food hit the spot, followed by ice cold beers. The TV didn't stay on for long after the meal. Necking like young kids progressed to grappling like college co-eds and finally consummated with steamy adult sex.

Denise approached sex as two good friends in a competition to see who could satisfy the other best. 'Best' meant bringing your partner to the highest possible level of excitement. It called for creativity and knowing when your partner was being most responsive to your manipulation.

With Bob she was afraid to show too much knowhow lest she come across as more skillful and less loving. She soon realized her concern was uncalled for. He easily asserted control of the situation. Straddling him, he nuzzled her breasts and found her 'g spot.' Their level of intimacy brought her to a highly intense orgasm.

As she came down from an incredible high, her concern was not that she would display too much knowhow, but whether she could muster a comeback in any way equivalent to what she had just experienced.

Again, there was no cause for concern. She found him eager to be under her control and readily responsive to a variety of her favorite forms of stimulation. His persistent erection was a source of excitement for both of them. He entered her from behind, holding her tightly, and they climaxed simultaneously.

Any doubts about physical compatibility were readily dispelled.

They lay together on his bed, now recovered from the high of a few moments ago.

"Bob, I keep waiting for something to go awry. Not that I'm a pessimist. It's just that everything we do seems to come off so right."

"I know what you're feeling, Denise, because the feeling is mutual. We're just beginning to know each other so there may yet be hills to climb. Let's just take them as they come and not anticipate trouble."

"I know you're right but I do have one issue which haunts me. I'd rather bring it up now than let it stew in my brain."

"Out with it, Denise. No bombs with a long fuse."

Denise took a long slow breath and then waded in. "Bob, you never married, for whatever reason. What if this fairytale of ours goes on and ripens to the point where people consider marriage and all that entails. Could you contemplate that? Or is it a step you can't imagine yourself ever taking?"

Denise anticipated a defensive reaction on Bob's part. Even worse, their first fight. Instead, Mr. Perfect, as she privately referred to him, never blinked.

"Denise, that's a fair question. My answer is simple. Yes, I can contemplate marriage. You've made that easy for me. So, take it off your worry list." He stopped and gave her a slight smile.

Denise was speechless for a moment. She decided to go with his answer and not pursue that subject any further.

"Bob, let's shower and return to planet earth. There's something mundane I want to talk to you about."

The shower was mostly about simply washing up. Their passion was spent so there was little play as they scrubbed each other's back.

Now, dressed in shorts and T-shirts, they ate ice cream sitting on the sofa.

"Okay, Denise, what's the mundane item you want to put out on the table?"

She related the story about reduced absenteeism at Sampson and her need to write an honors paper. She knew she'd get honest feedback.

"Sounds like a very good topic, Denise. It's original research. That's much better than a review of written articles and books. It's also more fun. The only drawback is that you may not find the answer."

"Thanks Bob. I really appreciate your assessment. I can deal with whatever outcome results. I agree that a clear answer may not be forthcoming. With or without a firm conclusion there'll be a story to tell. I'm going to pursue it. Now, let's scour Netflix and see if we can find something to watch that isn't about zombies, giant living things, or homicidal neighbors."

CHAPTER EIGHTEEN

Obtaining a sample of the powder accumulated on the exhaust fans wasn't difficult. Early one evening, Mitch went to the deserted chemical processing area. He found a tall, freestanding ladder which allowed workmen to do maintenance on the lofty ceiling, like changing light bulbs or repairs on the exhaust fans. He scraped some of the white powder into a small vial and put the ladder back where he found it.

A small analytic laboratory not far from Sampson had agreed to do the analysis for a modest sum. It would take no more than two days. This expense would be all his own. He had decided that his sleuthing in this matter would be kept secret. After dropping off the sample, and before driving home, he remained in his car and reflected on his findings and the theory he was beginning to formulate.

The powder was a key to the mystery. He was sure, even though there was absolutely no hard evidence. Workers breathed in fumes and became dependent on some chemical in the fumes. The dependence led them to return to the worksite for more fumes. He was no dummy. He'd learned about physical dependence in pharmacy school. It usually involved a drug, but he suspected that it could be any chronic exposure to a chemical.

He liked this theory. It explained the findings. Next he'd find out if there was a specific chemical in the powder that could reasonably be expected to cause physical dependence. He'd have to be a little patient.

When he finally pulled into his driveway at home it was like awakening from a trance. He had no recollection of driving home and could only wonder how he had managed to avoid any serious mishaps.

CHAPTER NINETEEN

Denise's father suggested that she use Mitchell Trent as her company resource to help her gain access to any files or personnel she might need to carry out her study. So, bright and early the next morning she was sitting outside Mitch's office waiting for him to arrive. His secretary said he had a clear calendar this morning so she would get in to see him without an appointment. Denise told her that she'd known Mitch almost her entire life since she was Larry Crandall's daughter. The secretary laughed and offered her a cup of coffee.

Mitch arrived and did a double take when he saw Denise. They hadn't seen each other in over a year but his recognition of her was instantaneous.

"Oh my god! What a surprise." They hugged each other and backed away smiling broadly.

"I never expected to see *you* when I walked in. It's great to see you, Denise. Come on in and fill me in on what's been going on in your life. Your dad and I hardly ever just sit and talk family."

Denise was pleased to see that he was so warmly disposed toward her. They went into his office and made themselves comfortable in his two soft leather easy chairs.

After a few minutes hearing about her recent career progress, Mitch moved the conversation onto her reason for the visit. "I know this isn't just a social call, Denise, though that would be just fine."

"You're right, Mitch, I'm here to ask for a small favor. My dad said you'd be the best person to open a few doors for me."

Denise related the background that led to this visit. "So you can see that I'm hoping to do some research and write my senior paper about the absenteeism matter here at Sampson."

Mitch was taken aback but managed to maintain a pleasant, good-natured façade. He wanted to squash her idea but didn't see an easy way to do that. He'd just be a helpful family friend until he could see how far she got with her project. Once he had the chemical analysis of the powder, he'd decide how best to preserve the secrecy he was intent on maintaining. Denise was only a potential problem at this point so there was no sense overreacting and setting off any alarm bells.

"Sure, Denise. I'd be pleased to help any way I can. Just keep me informed about your progress. It should be an interesting project for you and one that's very germane to the business degree you're about to receive. Now, let me hear about what you've been up to the past few years that isn't about your school life."

CHAPTER TWENTY

The call from Gardner Analytics was directed to Mitch's cell phone. His heart rate bumped up when he recognized the caller ID. The call was only informing him that the report was complete and ready for pick-up as he'd requested.

He left work and drove over to Gardner. The report was waiting for him at the reception desk. Back in his car he couldn't wait to tear open the envelope and read the report. It was all of one printed page with a copy of some chromatographic graphs. The powder was ninety-three percent pure with small amounts of various minor components. The dominant chemical had a very long name and was totally foreign to him. He'd anticipated this and had lined up a consultant pharmacologist in Denver. He'd chosen a person who had no connection to him or Sampson. Mitch had offered a generous fee for a very private phone consultation.

His call to Denver went straight to the consultant's office.

"Harry Stockman, here. I don't recognize your number, so please identify yourself."

"Dr. Stockman, I'm the person who called last week about a telephone consultation. I now have identified the chemical I need your help with."

Stockman didn't hesitate a moment. "Right. I recall you now. You said your name was Bertram Thomas but didn't say how you came to possess the powder in question. Look, why don't you just give me the name of the chemical and I'll get back to you in a day or two? Or better yet, send me a copy of the report you received from the analytic chemist. As I remember, you were primarily interested in information about human or animal interaction and effects. Am I right?"

"Yes, indeed. Maybe some additional questions will come up after I see your report. I'll put a check in the mail as soon as I receive it. You have my cellphone number. Okay, here's the chemical name. I'll email you a copy of the report today."

CHAPTER TWENTY-ONE

Studying together in a small one-bedroom apartment with a girl-friend brought old memories back for Bob. He was studying the material George O'Reilly had gathered for him about the mayor while Denise pored over the report from Sampson Industries that her mother had brought to her attention. Mitch had been very helpful, giving her a number of additional recent reports regarding products, contracts, and financial details of the company.

Bob and Denise saw each other almost every evening. Tonight they were having dinner at her parents' home in Scarsdale. Her mother had insisted on a second meeting with her daughter's new beau. She had to be convinced that Mr. Too-Good-To-Be-True really was all that Denise said he was. The young couple would Uber up to Westchester around seven.

Denise was getting deep into the business side of Sampson. The absenteeism data was intriguing. She could see several avenues to pursue, including interviews with a number of workers. It seemed like an ideal subject for her paper. Even with no paper hanging over her head, solving this mystery was the type of challenge she enjoyed.

The drive to Scarsdale gave Bob his first good look at the suburbs of Westchester County; some very prosperous and others less so. It was little different than the "burbs" north of San Francisco. Sure, the topography was different, but he felt very familiar with the homes and their setting. He was getting a feel for where Denise had grown up. Comfortable, but not showy.

They no sooner were out of the Uber car when the front door of the house opened and Elaine Crandall was coming down the front walk to embrace her daughter. Larry Crandall was only a few steps behind his wife, and hugged Denise with gusto while Elaine warmly greeted Bob.

"About time Denise let us meet you in the flesh, Bob. That brief intermission at *Carousel* was hardly enough to let us get to know you."

"Likewise, Elaine. I've been looking forward to this day ever since Denise and I began monopolizing each other's time. She also promised me a great meal."

Once inside the house, Bob noted it was larger and more graceful inside than one would suspect from viewing the outside. They made themselves comfortable in the living room and Larry saw to it that everyone had a drink in hand. Denise and Bob sat next to each other on the sofa.

Elaine wasted no time getting personal.

"Denise hasn't held back any information about you, Bob. We're impressed how you've done so much in your relatively short lifetime."

"Elaine, your daughter is one of a kind as far as I'm concerned. And that's after only a few weeks of getting to know each other. I don't think I'm telling you anything you don't know."

The evening progressed pleasantly with a host of stories about Denise's and Bob's childhood experiences and the obvious difference in their early lives. When they'd all had a fill of that, Denise gratefully changed the subject and brought up the matter of her Sampson project and the help she received from Mitch.

Larry exposed his relative ignorance of the matter, something Bob found peculiar since he and Mitch were co-owners of the company and had numerous opportunities to share that kind of information.

Bob continued the discussion of Denise's project and directed his comments to her father. "Larry, Denise has sunk her teeth into the matter and is now about to interview a number of the workers in the chemical processing part of your plant. I've encouraged her because I think there's a good story to tell here." There was little feedback from Larry.

On the drive back to New York, Denise was in a very buoyant mood.

"I was worried for a moment that my mother was going to try to steal you from me. She has a playful side that sometimes needs taming."

"She almost had me there for a moment. I enjoyed teetering between two Crandall women. Her beef bourguignon beats anything I've seen you cook so far, so don't get overconfident, Ms. Crandall."

CHAPTER TWENTY-TWO

Marge was ready with the list Denise had requested of employees who worked in the section with low absenteeism. She thanked Marge and waved to Mitch's empty chair.

"It's early for Mitch to get into the office. He prefers to work late. I'll tell him you picked up the list."

"Thanks, Marge. You're a great help."

"You're very welcome, Denise. Just one more thing. I'd appreciate you keeping me up to date on any progress you make on this matter. As the company HR officer, I'm more than a little interested in solving the mystery. I might even be able to help you interpret some of your findings."

"Thanks, Marge. That's a kind offer. I'll be sure to keep you in the loop if I'm lucky enough to create one."

They both laughed, shook hands, and Denise left with her package of information.

Left alone in the office, Marge reflected on how little interest Mitch had shown when she first brought the company report to his attention. Now here he was counseling this student in a detailed analysis of the situation. It seemed odd, but so was Mitch. As the Sampson HR person, she naturally was interested in whatever Denise uncovered. For some reason, Mitch had not encouraged any investigation on her part.

CHAPTER TWENTY-THREE

Mitch immediately recognized the number calling from Denver. Harry Stockman hadn't wasted any time getting back to him. The call came while he was driving home so he pulled into a convenient supermarket parking lot and accepted the call.

"Hello, Professor Stockman. Thanks for the prompt callback."

He fought to contain his excitement. He didn't want Stockman to sense any unusual level of interest. He wanted to keep their arrangement on a very mundane level.

"Well, Mr. Thomas, the compound you have in your possession is not a commercial preparation, but it bears a faint resemblance to a class of stimulants called methylxanthines. The chemical resemblance is quite superficial so it may or may not have any effects of that drug class. It nevertheless may have the potential to create physical dependence after prolonged exposure. I wouldn't be surprised if it elicited a mildly euphoric sensation. But here I'm only guessing since I know of no clinical work done with this compound. In short, you're flying blind if this compound was taken internally by a human."

"That's very useful information Dr. Stockman. I assume there would be some withdrawal symptoms if a person exposed to the compound abruptly stopped the exposure?"

"I can only speculate, but that seems reasonable. A short period off a drug, like several days, might not bother a patient who is physically dependent. Again, we're flying blind here. That kind of information comes from careful clinical trials that would also uncover other side effects. I guess I'm only able to give you speculative information, absent such a trial. I hope that's of some help."

"Professor, you've been most helpful. Your payment will be in the mail tonight. As I indicated when we first spoke, I may come back to you for additional help if specific questions come up. I'm very appreciative."

Mitch was even more excited than when he first took the call. Stockman didn't know of any clinical trials, but Mitchell Trent did. One was being carried out right here at Sampson without anyone realizing it. Well, one person did. Mitch Trent. And he intended to keep it that way.

As he began to put it all together, he considered the neat package of cause and effect. The compound obviously created a physical dependence; why else were the exposed workers so eager to be on the job? In addition, he knew they tolerated a few days away from the plant without significant symptoms of withdrawal. Euphoria? He didn't know about that, but wouldn't be surprised if that added to the attraction of the workplace. All in all, it was a neat package. He had the chemical's formula and could easily get the "recipe" for making it. What he didn't know was what to do with all this information. Somehow there had to be a way to convert that powder into greenbacks.

CHAPTER TWENTY-FOUR

The doorman at the building had been expecting Leslie. He ushered her into the rather garish elevator and the elevator operator took her to the tenth floor. The elevator opened into a small vestibule with only two doors. The operator indicated which door led to the Hillman apartment. Before she could knock the door was opened by a tall, good-looking man dressed casually in a V-neck sweater, button-down shirt, and slacks with loafers. Leslie was glad she'd dressed equally casual in a skirt and crewneck sweater.

"You must be Leslie. I'm Bob Hillman. Come on in."

He led her into a spacious living area with contemporary furniture and several framed posters from painting exhibitions on the walls.

"I rented it furnished and fortunately the previous tenant had good taste. Make yourself comfortable. Sit where it suits your needs for the interview. I'm in no hurry so we can chat a while before we get into the serious matter of the interview."

"That suits me fine. Can I call you Bob?"

"Of course. The more informal we are the better."

"I'd like to get to know you, Bob, so I can see how much personal info would go into the article based on the interview. Your profile on Google laid out the basics about you. I brought you a copy to read so you can tell me what's in it that's not accurate. You can also tell me what you'd add. This is just background of course, but sometimes that's useful. Take a minute to read it."

He gave it a serious perusal and handed it back to her.

"Nothing to add or subtract. It's a fair summary of my life. I own a large company, am very committed to pushing alternative energy, and have no illusions about the complexity of that path."

"The article has you forty-two years old and never married."

"Guilty as charged. I don't see a ring on your finger either, Leslie. But let's leave it at that. Now, how about that interview Leslie?"

The interview lasted more than an hour. Leslie found Bob easy to engage and he was very forthcoming. It was a pleasant hour for each of them.

"I think I have what I need, Bob. We can call it quits. If there's anything you think we didn't cover in enough detail, now's the time to add it."

"Nope. You got it all. I never saw you doze or appear to be drowning in details of energy production. I'm impressed. Now I hope you'll have lunch with me. I took the chance you'd say yes and bought some good kosher deli this morning. What do you say?"

"Who could turn down such an offer after an hour of interviewing? Lead me to it. The only thing that could spoil the offer would be rye bread with seeds. I prefer seedless."

"I couldn't risk a turndown so I got 'with seeds' and 'seedless.'"

They both had a good laugh and moved into the kitchen for lunch.

Leslie left the building feeling good about the interview. She couldn't help feeling captivated by Bob Hillman. What woman wouldn't? She tried to put that out of her mind. He didn't make a pass at her and kept the conversation over lunch on a purely friendly plane. All gentleman. Would he follow up with a call? He had her card, so he had her number.

She found herself hoping he would. She hadn't met a man who had this effect on her in quite some time.

Sitting in the living room, he tried to focus on the poster above the bar. He greatly admired Caravaggio and found his work a useful distraction when he wanted to put something out of his mind. His interview with the reporter had been disconcerting. She was very appealing, but there was no space in his life for another woman. He had to put her out of his mind.

CHAPTER TWENTY-FIVE

The Neurology Clinic at Columbia Presbyterian Hospital was, as usual, totally booked for the morning. Doctor Christine Dinsmore was the Clinic staff person supervising several neurology and rotating medical residents. One of the neurology residents had just presented a case to her.

The patient, James Healy, was a fifty-three-year-old factory worker who noted numbness in his feet and stumbled several times in the past week. His history and exam were normal with the exception of a moderate loss of sensation to light touch and pin prick in both feet. He also had a diminished sense of position in his feet.

The patient and his wife were seated in the exam room while Dr. Dinsmore and the resident stood before them. Dr. Dinsmore saw no reason to alarm the patient. She wanted time to review the details of the case before making any pronouncement. She saw the case as a very good learning experience for the neurology resident who would likely see plenty of peripheral nerve disorders in his future practice.

"Mr. Healy, you have some loss of sensation in your feet. You knew that. We need to find the cause and, if possible, change something in your life that may be contributing to the problem. I don't expect to see any rapid change so you should go about your normal life while we look for any causative factors. We'll see you back here in two weeks. Do you have any questions for us?"

Mrs. Healy spoke up. "How serious is this, Dr. Dinsmore?"

"I don't want to make too much of it, but it is of some concern. Let us do some brainstorming and see what we can come up with. We have your home phone and Dr. Littlefield, the resident who examined you, may call for additional information before your next visit. Okay? We'll see you in two weeks."

The Healys left.

"Dr. Littlefield, we'll need a detailed work and drug history. Do some deep reading and let's have a plan ready for the Healys when we see them at their next visit."

Dr. Dinsmore had been somewhat less than forthcoming with the Healys. She'd seen a number of cases like this and they rarely made a reasonable recovery. The causes differed but the outcomes were depressingly bleak.

CHAPTER TWENTY-SIX

In just four days, Denise had managed to interview half a dozen workers on her list. The stories she heard were monotonously similar. Each worker enjoyed his job (they were all male) and looked forward to going to work each day. Weekends, when the plant was closed, were spent in rather normal family activities. One wife complained her husband was a bit irritable by Sunday evening but it wasn't a problem for them. All in all the workers were happy in their jobs and that seemed to account for their strong record of attendance.

So what's the big deal? thought Denise. For some reason this unusual record of attendance was a new phenomenon. In the previous year, she noted on reviewing old records, there was a more "normal" pattern of attendance. Three months ago the change had taken place.

"So what else had changed?" she asked her next interviewee. He said the team's jobs were unchanged. They had begun working on a new

product about four or five months previous, but their individual responsibilities were the same.

Denise had found at least one change in the plant to mull over.
The group was handling a new product. Now she'd write up a progress
report at her apartment and then get ready for her evening with Bob.

CHAPTER TWENTY-SEVEN

Mitch had the "recipe" for making the product that emitted the fumes. It was clearly spelled out in the contract with the company they were working for. He knew he could assemble the necessary equipment to brew the compound. Once that was done he would be able to manufacture it in quantity.

The biggest challenge would be finding a distributer for the product. Here he realized he would have to accept the harsh reality that some drug dealer would take a sizable share of the sale profits. He needed help and couldn't afford to be greedy.

It occurred to him that he would have to convince a dealer that his product was effective. He was unsure how to do this. Stockman's report was a start and, coupled with the actual effects noted in the workplace, would have to suffice as a starter.

He was growing increasingly optimistic about the future. This unexpected stroke of good fortune had fallen into his lap. His major concern was keeping this secret very close to his vest.

Marge was probably getting anxious at their rendezvous site since he was already ten minutes late. He called her cell and told her he was on the way. He was feeling very good.

CHAPTER TWENTY-EIGHT

Denise was waiting outside Marge's office bright and early at eight in the morning. Marge invited her in and made coffee for the two of them.

"What brings you in here at this hour, Denise?"

"Remember, Marge, I said I'd keep you up to date on my project. You've been very helpful to me so I'm following through. Here's a progress report on what I've been able to learn so far. I think it's interesting even if it doesn't solve the puzzle. I'd appreciate any thoughts you may have after reading it." She handed a bound document to Marge.

"I'll certainly read it and get back to you as soon as I finish it. We can get together over dinner and discuss what you found."

"Sounds good to me, Marge. I think I uncovered something that may be a clue to what's going on. It's very preliminary and lacking a clear connection, but I couldn't find a helluva lot to work with."

The two women dropped Sampson talk and moved on to more personal matters. Neither heard Mitch enter his office next door so both were surprised when he came into Marge's office, unaware that Denise was there.

"Good morning, Marge. Whoa. Hello, Denise. What a surprise. What brings you here so early?"

Marge jumped in "Denise brought me a progress report on her project. I offered to read it and give her some feedback."

"Great idea, Marge, but I want to be the first to read it." Mitch said it with a big grin, but behind the grin was a concern that his secret might be endangered. If Denise had really found anything worrisome, he didn't want the circle of informed people widened even a tiny bit. He reached over Marge's desk and snapped up what he rightly suspected was the report in question.

"I'll read it tonight and you can have it back tomorrow, Marge. As for you Denise, please keep me in the loop, too. I'm very interested in what you may find."

"Sure, Mitch, I wasn't trying to go around you. It's just that Marge has been so helpful I wanted to show her I consider her a co-worker on the project. Next time I'll bring two copies of the report."

Mitch wanted to keep this episode with the report very low key. Inching toward the door, he gave the two women a broad smile and put his hands up as if to say "no harm done."

"Hey, Denise, sorry I can't stay and schmooze. Got a research committee meeting waiting for me." With that Mitch and the report were out the door and down the hall. Marge and Denise looked at each other a bit surprised.

"That's the most interest he's shown, Denise, since the initial company report came out. I couldn't get a rise out of him when I first called it to his attention."

"C'est la vie, Marge. That's a man for you."

CHAPTER TWENTY-NINE

Mitch didn't go to any meeting. Instead he went to his car in the parking lot where he could read Denise's report in private. He didn't know what to expect but he knew she was very bright and may have begun to put some of the puzzle pieces together.

It was a very dangerous report. She clearly had zeroed in on the new product as having some connection to the lack of absenteeism. The connection was pure speculation, but it pointed in a direction he didn't want her to go. She was barely into the project and was already threatening his goldmine. She had to be stopped. There also was no way Marge would ever see the report.

He had just stumbled onto the report by coming in unusually early. A stroke of luck, but now he was faced with a threat he had to eliminate. He thought for a moment. So, what if she even nailed down the exact cause of the issue just as he had done? He had the formula, could assemble the equipment to manufacture the compound in secret, and was going to link up with a dealer he kept at arm's length. Why should he care if Sampson halted production because the process created fumes that affected the workers? So, what if Sampson did the venting update on an accelerated schedule? He was prepared to pursue his find on a track apart from Sampson Industries.

CHAPTER THIRTY

York Chemical or YC was headquartered in downtown Yonkers. The offices were housed on the top floor of an unpretentious three-story building sitting between a moving company warehouse and an abandoned movie theatre. A number of nearby businesses were no longer active and 'for lease' signs were growing yellow in several storefronts.

Oscar Gleason's office was in the rear of the York office complex. His title as president was clearly displayed on the door. The depressed neighborhood was a perfect setting for York, a company not seeking any notoriety. The offices were well-appointed, considering the outward appearance of the building.

Manny Rufalo reported to his boss that something was stirring at Sampson that might need attention. Gleason was a calm but deadly serious boss who liked to keep his operation running like a fine-tuned motor.

Manny realized he was bringing some uncertainty into Gleason's carefully run operation and couldn't be sure what reaction he'd elicit.

"Our man on the inside said the contract is running smoothly, Oscar. The product is being produced on schedule. It meets our testing standards and, after being transported to our warehouse, the final distillate we prepare is fully up to our expectations. Our street dealers report no problems. The product is mixed with several different drugs and keeps our profit margin high."

Gleason continued to give Manny his undivided attention even though this preamble would make a less placid man scream at him to get to the point.

"Well, our man on the work crew says the Sampson COO, Mitch Trent, showed up at the worksite recently and showed unusual interest in the site's activity. Then the night watchman casually mentioned to our guy that Trent had visited the area one night. Putting two and two together our man believes the COO may be onto something about the process and could cause trouble."

"Okay, Manny, I read you. That's good observation on our man's part. Tell him from me I said that, and give him a little something extra this week. Then meet with this COO and convince him he doesn't wanna get involved where he hasn't been invited. Don't land heavy on him. I don't think he's trouble. We're not looking to make any big waves. The setup is a sweet one with a legit company making our not so legit product."

"I read you, boss. I'll take care of it."

Oscar Gleason had no background in chemistry. After completing a lackluster high school education in Tennessee, he moved to New York City to seek his fortune. Lacking good looks or any special skills, the best he could come up with was a street worker for a numbers racket in the decaying South Bronx. He made himself available for dishing out punishment to customers who reneged on obligations. Oscar had never been comfortable with the role of an enforcer, but that was the "career path" laid open for him. He swore to himself that when he was in a position to hire his own enforcer he'd turn those unpleasant chores over to him in a hurry. Violence was not a part of his nature.

His star rose in the organization when he personally took out an especially dangerous pair of Serbian competitors and left no trail back to his boss. These were his only killings and the fact that he left no trail was more a matter of self-preservation than loyalty to his boss. Nevertheless, his reward was the opportunity to run a small commercial chemical company in Yonkers that also produced product for marketing on the street. He never looked back. When Sampson Industries proposed becoming a silent partner, it offered York an avenue to new product. This established Oscar as a respected operator in the New York drug trade.

The head of the organization that dominated the New York drug trade saw the York-Sampson partnership as a very small piece of the organization. It didn't merit much oversight and satisfied the organization's debt to Gleason. Alyssa Ross, undisputed head of the organization, was personally responsible for granting Gleason permission to set up and run the York operation. Eric Dinsmore, her attorney, was only informed about her decision in passing during their regular luncheon meeting. He took little note of her action but put York on the organization chart. No regular reporting contact was established between York and the organization.

A young Italian from a rough neighborhood in Brooklyn was referred to Oscar by a sister of his wife. Manny Rufalo. His background was similar to Oscar's with the exception that he had no distaste for violence. In an interview, Oscar saw in Manny the traits he needed: cold-blooded willingness to carry out harsh tasks and strong loyalty to whoever lifted him out of the street.

Manny had been raised by his older brother, Vincent, in a household missing a father who had been killed by DEA agents in a drug bust. His mother was mentally impaired following a severe beating administered by a boyfriend. Vincent imparted to Manny the street smarts neces-

71

sary for survival and eventual success in the drug world that was the principal industry in their section of Brooklyn. He left high school after two years and was running drugs for various dealers when he was referred to Oscar Gleason.

CHAPTER THIRTY-ONE

The party at Joann Lightner's loft apartment in the village was still going strong after midnight. The crowd included a lot of Joann's good friends living in the New York area. Denise Crandall and Chris Dinsmore were two of her friends who also happened to be close to each other from high school days. Denise was there with Bob Hillman and Chris with her husband, Eric Dinsmore. The two guys hit it off and were soon deep in a discussion of the president's energy policy.

Denise and Chris were like sisters. They immediately brought each other up to date on events in their lives.

"Chris, I want to hear how life goes for a junior neurologist at Columbia. We see so little of each other since you joined the staff of that august department. I miss you."

"I feel exactly the same, Denise. I hope we can do something about that. Anyway, I want to hear all about that guy you brought with you. Is there something serious going on? Over the phone you sounded unusually upbeat last time we talked. That was over a week ago."

The two women found seats in a corner of the big living area, leaned into each other, and shut out the crowd around them. An intimate conversation kept them engrossed for the next half hour. A waiter came by and briefly broke the spell to offer them drinks. When Chris resumed the conversation, she was talking about her work.

"I really like what I do. I see a great variety of pathology in the clinic. It's stimulating and sometimes rewarding. Other times it can be a bit depressing. Many of the patients have problems for which I have no good answer. They want a cure and there may be none. Sometimes it's worse and I have to give them the news that the problem not only won't be solved but will actually keep progressing.

"For instance, recently I saw a fiftyish male with nerve damage. Sensation was significantly impaired in his feet. The handwriting on the wall suggested a dismal future. I didn't want to offer the grim prognosis so I held back and put off that conversation. My resident did a careful history and found out that he's a blue-collar worker in a chemical plant. His livelihood will be at stake. That's the kind of sad stuff you see in neurology practice. So much for my work experience. You shouldn't let me go on like this. Let's get back to you and your West Coast sweety."

"There's not much to tell. We really hit it off and find it a bit frightening to contemplate the future. I'm happier than I've ever been, Chris. I keep wondering how something this wonderful could have been the result of pure chance. I'm beginning to sound like a mystic and that's the time to change the subject. Okay? Let me tell you about the project I've just begun working on for my honors award."

CHAPTER THIRTY-TWO

Early evening sunshine was still lighting the parking lot as Mitch headed for his car. He was consumed with thoughts about his discovery at the plant. A well-dressed man in sport coat and slacks was walking behind him and caught up to him just as he reached his car. Mitch heard his name and turned to see who had called him. The man smiled, now sure he had the person he wanted to talk to.

"Do I know you?" Mitch didn't recognize Manny but wasn't alarmed at being approached by a stranger in the parking lot.

"I don't think so, Mr. Trent, but we need to talk. This is a good place to do it so I hope you'll allow me to introduce myself and ask that you hear me out." The stranger seemed friendly and gave off no threatening vibes.

"I guess I can give you a few minutes. You have me at a disadvantage since I have no idea what you want of me."

"Good. I'm Manny Rufalo and I work at York Chemical. You know us since we have contracts with you to make some of our additives. That's what I want to talk to you about."

"Couldn't this best be done in my office? My secretary will set up a time for us to meet and discuss any concerns you may have regarding the contracts."

"What I have to say won't take but a few minutes, so I think we can do our business here and now."

Mitch sensed something less than friendly in Manny's tone of voice and facial expression. The smile was gone and his face was now unreadable.

"You seem to be showing a sudden interest in one of our products. I'm here to ask you to shelve that interest. Just drop it. My company would prefer you go back to the way you were before this sudden interest took hold of you. That's my message. If you're fully understanding and agreeable we see no need for further discussion."

Mitch was beginning to get the drift of this conversation. How did this guy know about his recent investigation? He was being given a warning. And it wasn't about an additive they were making for a commercial wood preservative. He needed to end this meeting and digest the take-home message.

"I think I'm agreeable."

"Then let's shake on it." Manny extended his hand and firmly shook hands with Mitch. As fast as that, Manny turned away and headed toward a waiting car not fifty feet away.

Mitch watched the car drive off and then got into his own car. He didn't start the engine right away. He sat there and tried to read the implications of the message he'd been given. What a fool he'd been. His scheme was too good to be true—because it was. He was an amateur in the drug business and the professionals had just told him to get lost.

CHAPTER THIRTY-THREE

Word leaked back to Eric Dinsmore in his Manhattan law office that some ripples had been seen on the pond. Drumbeats may not have been heard but news traveled from Yonkers that York Chemical was experiencing some hiccups. The organization he worked for was very sensitive to "ripples" and liked to head off problems before they actually materialized.

After hearing the few details of what sounded like a very small matter, he decided to include it in the weekly report he'd be giving to Alyssa Ross, the president, this afternoon. Her office was just a short walk down the hall on the same floor.

Eric seated himself in the waiting room of the Ross-Wagner president. The privately held company owned a fleet of cargo container ships. It was the third largest container ship company in the western world and was highly profitable. Alyssa Ross was the sole owner, having inherited the company from her father, Oliver Ross, upon his death near-ly nine years ago. Thomas Wagner had been an early co-owner long be-fore it became the mammoth company it was today. He had died young and Oliver Ross had bought out his heirs at a generous price. Wagner's name was maintained on the company's letterhead to keep Oliver, and now Alyssa, from being too conspicuous.

Big as Ross-Wagner was, it was only a part of Alyssa's portfolio. Her other asset was an illegal drug empire that had been instrumental in raising the funds to build the cargo ship company. The shipping company provided an excellent respectable cover for Alyssa. The drug empire had been built from the bottom up by Oliver Ross in the most ruthless man-ner. The two disparate organizations had been passed on to her by her father who saw her, his only heir, as fully capable of carrying on the fami-ly business.

As a drug kingpin in the New York metropolitan area, she ruled with a firm hand, quite different than the Forbes 500 image she cultivat-ed and maintained with a gracious, generous, and warm-hearted lifestyle.

Born in Boston, educated at Smith College and Harvard Business School, Alyssa's schooling gave no indication that she would be an equal success at both legitimate and illegitimate business. Her marriage to Vic-tor Brandt, a respected surgeon, was a stable one of twenty-seven years and had produced two children who now were beginning careers, one as a lawyer and the other as an economist. In short, her public profile was pure vanilla. The only thing that stood out was her wealth, but that was attributed to Ross-Wagner with no hint that drug traffic had anything to do with her material wealth.

Eric Dinsmore was her attorney and "fixer." She was his only cli-ent.

He entered the president's office and waited for an invitation to sit. Alyssa, just turned fifty, was wearing a navy suit and pale yellow shirt open at the neck. She was rather serious in demeanor and not unattrac-tive. She wore her brown hair in a pageboy style not unlike that she wore at Smith thirty years ago. She sat behind a large mahogany desk that was crowded with papers.

"Eric, it's nice to see you." Alyssa got up to greet her attorney. "What bad news do you bring me today? I guess I always hope that you'll surprise me and bring me some uplifting news I can laugh about with you. From the look on your face I don't think today is that day. Let's hear what you have."

"Nothing catastrophic, Alyssa. Our small plant in Yonkers, York Chemical, Oscar Gleason's shop, is worried about possible exposure of their drug production. Nothing is on the verge of happening but I wanted to alert you to the possibility of future trouble. I know you like to be aware of any impending problem."

He paused and confessed that he only knew a few scraps of information.

"The problem is centered in that company they quietly partnered with, Sampson Industries. I think it's under control for the moment, but I'm not sure there's final closure. I'll keep tabs on the matter until it's wrapped up."

"I do appreciate that sketchy update, Eric. You do just that. Keep an eye on the matter and keep me in the loop."

"Shall do, Alyssa."

With that he sensed the meeting was over and left without further conversation.

CHAPTER THIRTY-FOUR

Mount Vernon is an immediate suburb of New York City. Cross the street from the northern Bronx and you're in Mount Vernon. The small four square miles had seen better days. Affluence had moved further north to Scarsdale and now Chappaqua and beyond. The Tyler family lived in the oldest part of the city in a two-story wood-frame house. They occupied the top floor.

Denise had made the interview appointment for 7:00 p.m. She now climbed the squeaking stairs and was met by a smiling Andrea Tyler.

Her husband Ethan had worked at Sampson for nearly twenty years.

The interview was similar to her previous six. Ethan was a happy employee who looked forward to getting to the plant and doing his tasks on the product line. His only issue was his feet. He was finding it difficult to keep his footing when the floor in the work area became wet. His wife had noticed he tripped around the house and took more time on the stairs, going up or down. He seemed to watch his footing very carefully.

Denise followed up on this. "Is there a problem with your feet, Mr. Tyler? Is this something you need to bring to a doctor's attention?"

Mrs. Tyler was quick to jump in here. "Virginia Healy told me her husband Jim was having a similar problem. Jim works with Ethan. He saw a doctor at Columbia just last week. I've been after Ethan to see someone about this problem but he's stubborn."

"So, Mr. Healy works with Ethan at Sampson?" asked Denise.

Ethan answered the question. "Yep, works right alongside me and has for over ten years."

"How long have you noticed this problem with your feet, Mr. Tyler?"

"Just this past month or so I'd guess. It seems to be getting worse but it doesn't keep me from carrying out my job. I never miss a day."

Denise thought she had all the information she came for. "I think that about wraps up my interview. I want to thank you for your help. You've been very kind. Oh, yes. Did Mrs. Healy give you the name of her husband's doctor at Columbia?"

Mrs. Tyler dug around in her purse and produced a card. "Here it is. Doctor Christine Dinsmore."

Denise was stunned to hear her friend's name. She thought back to her conversation with Chris at the Lightner party. Chris had told her about a patient she'd seen with a neuropathy, a nerve disorder in his feet. Surely that was the Healy case. Denise sensed that she may have stumbled onto something important, though not clearly related to her primary purpose for interviewing Ethan Tyler. She couldn't wait to write up her second progress report. Two workers in the same area with a similar problem.

CHAPTER THIRTY-FIVE

Denise and Chris took their Chinese takeout with them into Central Park. They found an empty bench along the bike path. The late afternoon sky was preparing for a golden sunset. Both women enjoyed this time of day and tried to have dinner together as often as possible, which wasn't very often.

"I couldn't believe my ears when Mrs. Tyler told me about her husband's co-worker who had a similar problem with his feet. And then she fished your card out of her purse. Unbelievable. Something is going on that has to fit together with the absenteeism issue I'm researching."

"It could be a coincidence, Denise, but two in the same workplace certainly raises a red flag. Have you visited the workplace? I think that's got to be next on your agenda. It certainly raises the possibility of some kind of toxin that's beginning to cause a problem. How that relates to your study is murky, but I bet it's connected."

"I'm seeing Mitch, Mr. Trent, tomorrow so I'll discuss it with him. It sounds like a problem for OSHA. I feel bad about dropping this bomb on him but it sounds too serious to be ignored."

"Keep me posted. Maybe I'll visit the plant with you. It sounds like Mr. Tyler will be coming to visit me very soon. But, let's change the subject to something more optimistic. Like, how goes it with Mr. Perfect? Are you two still walking on clouds or has your mom stolen him away from you?"

"I know you're kidding, Chris, but sometimes I think my mom is a bit jealous of her daughter. She did actually discover Bob. But in answer to your question, we're still in the cloud stage and enjoying every minute of it. I even had the nerve to ask this lifelong bachelor if he'd ever consider marriage or if he was a confirmed bachelor."

"You didn't!"

"I did, and he said the thought had recently crossed his mind. With that, I have to go now and leave you panting in anticipation of the next episode."

They walked their lunchboxes to the trash bin, hugged, and headed off in opposite directions.

CHAPTER THIRTY-SIX

Mitch sat in his office still wondering what options he had regarding the product Manny had taken out of his eager hands. He also was wondering how he could continue to go along helping Denise as she sniffed around Sampson and ran the risk of getting into Manny's crosshairs. He'd have to wait until this morning's update from her to determine if she was getting dangerously close to figuring out what was going on in the plant.

At eight thirty sharp, Denise blew into his outer office with her usual buoyant greeting. "Good morning, Mitch. I brought coffee for the two of us and some pastries as well. There's cream and sugar in the bag, so help yourself."

"Denise, you really know how to win a guy over."

"I'm glad you're sitting, Mitch, because some of my information may knock you over. It's all contained in this report." She handed him a report several stapled pages long.

"First, I want to tell you about the interviews I conducted with a number of the workmen. There were no surprises and no clues regarding the amazing run of low absenteeism. But there was one interesting finding. Ethan Tyler, a long timer on the Sampson staff, is having some difficulty with his feet. He stumbles and has some uncertainty in his gait."

"I'm sorry to hear that, Denise, but what has that to do with the price of tea in China? Excuse my old figure of speech."

"Well, there is more to this story. I have a friend, a neurologist at Columbia, and she's recently seen a patient with the same problem. Curious thing is that her patient is a co-worker with Ethan Tyler in the chemical manufacturing area. It can't just be coincidence. There may be something in the area that's toxic, so I'm bringing this sad story to you. It sounds like an OSHA matter."

"That's great detective work, Denise. I'm very concerned. I'm glad you brought it to me so I can take the necessary steps to bring in OSHA and see how we can fix the problem."

He was on guard, quickly sizing up the issues and formulating a plan of action. First he had to limit Denise's role here and keep her from spreading the story any further. He assumed her doctor friend was aware of the matter. Second, he saw an opportunity to ingratiate himself with Manny and company and turn this to his advantage.

"Thanks again, Denise. I'll carry it on from here, but I'd appreciate it if you would keep the matter to yourself and put your study on hold until I can review it with the OSHA office. I think this kind of industrial investigation is best carried out quietly and not in the glare of a public spotlight."

"I have no problem with that, Mitch, even though it'll delay the paper I'm working on. I'll ask my friend at Columbia to likewise keep a lid on it until you signal me that we can talk about it with others."

"For my information, what is your friend's name in case the OSHA people want to contact her?"

"She's Doctor Christine Dinsmore."

"Thanks, Denise. I'm gonna dive right in and make some phone calls. I should have news for you in a few days. And thanks again for coming to me with the finding."

CHAPTER THIRTY-SEVEN

Mitch called York Chemical and asked to be connected to Manny Rufalo, still a bit unsure how to capitalize on the insider info. Manny answered on the second ring. "Manny here. What's up, Mr. Trent?"

Mitch spelled out the problem for Manny and wondered how he would react.

"If it's okay with you I'll call you Mitch and you can call me Manny. Thanks for the heads up, Mitch. That's a critical piece of information. I'm going to talk to my boss now. We'll put our heads together and come up with a strategy for coping with your news. You did the right thing in keeping a lid on it. We'll be sure to show our gratitude. Just be patient. My boss is very clever so I'm sure he'll put together a plan. Don't be surprised if it includes you. You're an insider now, so be ready. I'll be back to you later today. Ciao." Manny hung up.

Manny met with Oscar in the boss's office. For some reason, Manny always felt uneasy in Oscar's presence even though the headman had never threatened Manny. Oscar's calm demeanor was off-putting but had to be a façade.

Manny laid out the facts as related to him by Mitch. Oscar's face gave no hint of what he thought about the potential threat. He asked Manny for his opinion about how to resolve the problem. Oscar always asked Manny to lead off. This clever, tactful manner gave Manny a feeling of importance. Oscar believed this made Manny a better lieutenant; one who believed he was respected by his leader.

"I think the two women have to go, Oscar. I think Mitch can be trusted because he wants a place in our organization, and a piece of the pie. He'll earn it. The operation we're concerned with at Sampson should be moved to a better ventilated part of the shop and a new work crew put in place. This will allow the workflow to continue. The product will only be temporarily affected and the medical problem in the two workers will either slow or be halted. Obviously I'm no expert on this nerve thing, but we can get some expert help if need be. That's my opinion. I thought about it a lot last night. One last thing. I'd move very rapidly since we're trying to keep a tight lid on the information."

"Sounds like a carefully considered plan, Manny. What about OSHA?"

"I'd keep them out of this as long as possible. By cleaning up the worksite we may head them off at the pass, so to speak."

Oscar now weighed in with his characteristic unemotional monotone.

"You mentioned two women who had to go. I agree. The manner of elimination should be different for each. Their removal should not imply any common thread. I suggest one be eliminated in a very mundane manner and the other merely disappear. This Mitch fellow is not to be privy to any part of this plan."

"Yes, Oscar. I agree. He'll be kept in the dark but will have to be the main mover in transferring the operation to another part of the plant.

He'll also have to sit on the notification of OSHA until we think it's absolutely necessary."

"Good work, Manny."

CHAPTER THIRTY-EIGHT

Mitch needed something to reduce his tension. This morning had been nerve-wracking, to say the least. Into his office walked Marge, on the way to her own office, but eager to share a cup of coffee with him.

"How's the day lookin,' Mitch?"

"It's looking better since you stopped in."

Marge smiled at the compliment and Mitch saw just the thing to calm his nerves.

"Why don't we move our lunch date up a day, Marge? We can drive out to that inn on the Sound we were talking about the other day. Maybe even check out the thread count on their sheets. How's that sound?"

"Great! I think I can reschedule my afternoon office meetings. Your proposal, Mr. Trent, offers the opportunity for creative thinking.

That's always a good business strategy. Let's say one o'clock at your car in the parking lot."

"I'm glad to see you so flexible, Marge."

"By the way, Mitch, you never did give me back my copy of Denise's report. I also bet she dropped off a follow-up report recently. Did she?"

"Let's discuss this over lunch, Marge. There's a wrinkle we need to iron out regarding Denise's study."

Mitch saw a potential problem here. Marge didn't know what was in the reports she hadn't read, but her curiosity was a threat. She could always call Denise and request her own update. That would place Marge in jeopardy. He would have to steer her away from any contact with Denise.

CHAPTER THIRTY-NINE

Very early morning, the jogging track in Central Park saw few joggers. Manhattan was barely lit by the rising sun at just before six.

Harry Cowans, an investment banker on his regular run in the park, enjoyed the nearly deserted track. It allowed him to envision the trades he had in mind before the market opened. Markets in Asia had given him some useful information to move on.

As he moved along at a quick pace, hoping to do a full four miles this morning, he was distracted by a colorful object behind a bush on his right. He slowed and went back a few yards to take a closer look. The body of a woman lying face down, dressed in running clothes, was a shock. He knelt down next to her and could see no sign of life. Her eyes were open but not seeing. Her running shorts were down around her ankles, but there were no obvious signs of trauma. He stood up, dialed

911 on his cell, gave the operator his location, and agreed to stay with the body until the police arrived.

In less than five minutes a police car drove up on the road parallel to the track. The two officers took down what little information he could provide relevant to the body behind the bush. The officers didn't disturb what was a probable crime scene. They allowed Cowans to go along his way. Ten minutes later a homicide detail arrived. Lieutenant Claudia Gomes took charge of the scene. A forensic crew was not far behind. They photographed the body and carefully searched the area for footprints and any other potentially useful evidence. Only then did Gomes turn over the body.

The victim was an attractive blond Caucasian woman, thirty to forty years old. There was no immediate cause of death she could identify although her conjunctivas were bloodshot, suggesting strangulation. A runner's wallet on her upper left arm was removed and gave all the identifying information they needed. Denise Crandall, age thirty-two, living at 67 West 92nd Street. Apparently she was a graduate student at Columbia. A careful search of the area failed to disclose any clues to a possible suspect.

Leslie had picked up the police call for a homicide and hustled up to the crime scene in Central Park. She found herself in a small group of newspaper people who had picked up the same call. The police weren't giving out much information, just enough for a small story in the next day's early edition.

Gomes thought it odd that no keys were found, either in the runner's wallet or at the crime scene. Surely the runner would need a key to get into her building and apartment unless she had a roommate or husband to let her in. This information was not shared with the reporters.

The phone number in the runner's wallet to call in an emergency was a Westchester number and not a phone in Manhattan. This suggested she lived alone and made absence of a key more unusual. One other number in her wallet was for a cellphone listed for Christine

Dinsmore. The body was placed in a body bag to be driven to the morgue, where an autopsy would determine the cause of death. Detective Gomes would make the painful call to the emergency number listed on the ID card in her wallet. She also decided to go to the apartment listed in the wallet and satisfy her curiosity about the absent key.

The apartment at 92nd Street was easily identified at the mailbox. She rode the elevator to the sixth floor and rang the bell at the apartment. No one answered and the door was locked. The doorman was also the building super. He was eager to cooperate with the police, and before opening the door to the apartment indicated that Miss Crandall was an ideal tenant who lived alone.

Lieutenant Gomes and two uniformed officers searched the apartment and could only comment on the tenant's concern for order and cleanliness. Gomes was still puzzled by the missing key. All indications were that she lived alone, just as the super said. It was unlikely a friend had been in the apartment when the runner left and the friend was expected to be there when she returned. There would be no need for a key on her return.

Okay. Then where was the key in the apartment if she hadn't gone out with it? Still no key. And one more thing. There was no computer on her desk. There was a connection for a computer but no computer was in the apartment. That was oddity number two. So, her key was taken by her assailant who then entered her apartment and lifted the computer. And left the apartment in immaculate condition with no obvious other theft. For Gomes, this just didn't add up, but she had no other scenario to work with.

The medical examiner took a skull x-ray and identified an occipital skull fracture. Her upper airway was also fractured, consistent with strangulation. The all too common combination of findings suggested head trauma to incapacitate the vic followed by manual strangulation to end her life. Inspection for evidence of rape revealed semen in the vaginal vault. A sample was taken for DNA analysis. There was minimal evidence of trauma in the vulvar-vaginal area, suggesting sexual penetration while the vic was unconscious or dead. That would be consistent with the lowered running shorts. Consensual sexual activity hours before the attack could not be excluded.

It was estimated that the time of death was six to twelve hours before the body was discovered. The woman in running clothes was probably assaulted while running the previous evening.

CHAPTER FORTY

The death of Denise shattered her parents. Elaine was inconsolable. Larry was mute, trying to bring Elaine back into the world of the living. Bob was having a hard time keeping himself from joining Elaine in unmitigated grief. He'd gotten the news when he called Elaine to ask if she'd heard from Denise who wasn't answering his calls. Larry had taken the call and given Bob the brutal news as best he could. Bob was finding it difficult to accept that Denise was no more. Just like that. Any future they may have envisioned together evaporated in one day.

The police wrote off her death as a rape ending in a murder. There were no suspects and no clues to follow up. It wasn't the first case like this they had seen. The semen DNA didn't match any DNA in their files, nor did it match Bob's DNA in a voluntary blood sample.

96

The funeral was attended by many teary-eyed friends and rela-
tives. The graveside ceremony was more of the same. No words from a
clergyman could dispel the heartache that pervaded the occasion. Leslie
attended the church service and identified Bob Hillman along with the
distraught parents and younger brother. The parents were too shattered
for her, a stranger, to approach.

She went up to Bob and offered her sympathy. From the sadness
written on his face she knew that he and Denise must have been very
close. Maybe that explained the silence that followed her interview with
him. He recognized her and thanked her for the solace she offered. Leslie
came away with a feeling of genuine sadness even though she never knew
Denise.

Bob tried to pick out Denise's friend Chris in the crowd, but
strangely, she was not in attendance. That was the one thing he'd always
remember from the funeral. He tried calling her using the cellphone
number Denise had given him in the event he couldn't reach Denise. No
luck. He tried the Neurology Department at Columbia and they too
were at a loss to reach Chris. Eric, her husband, was also puzzled by
Chris's disappearance. He promised to call when she returned.

Bob cut short his venture in New York and made plans to return
to San Francisco. He had no enthusiasm for the project he'd been nurtur-
ing for several years. Losing Denise had sapped his energy and drained his
enthusiasm for life in general. When Denise had asked him about his willingness to ever consider marriage he had given her a heartfelt thumbs up.
They had both considered that a giant step forward in their relationship.

One month later, back in San Francisco, Bob's brooding was
slowly fading. Even this monstrous loss would recede into the past. Denise would never be forgotten, but her death would not keep him from
resuming his life.

BOOK TWO

CHAPTER ONE

San Francisco's late fall weather was a monotonous grey sky and frequent light rain. Today was no exception. Bob sat in an easy chair in his living room, reading a book about John Marshall and the early days of the Supreme Court. It had been some time since he attempted to do any serious reading.

The funeral still stuck in his mind. He couldn't shake it. It was misery fully realized. One thing continued to rise up whenever he let his mind drift back to those terrible days. It was strange what you remember most clearly out of a welter of memories. He still saw himself searching the faces at the graveside for Chris Dinsmore. How could she not be there?

This thought continued to plague him. Yet what could he do? It had been one month since the funeral and he still came back to Chris's absence. He reached for the telephone and called New York information.

"Hello, I'm trying to reach the homicide division of the New York City Police Department."

After a short pause a recorded voice gave him a telephone number and offered to dial it for a small charge. He gave his assent.

The phone was answered after many rings. A friendly voice identified the site as the homicide division and asked how she could help him.

"I'm trying to reach Lieutenant Claudia Gomes."

After a brief delay a voice came on and identified herself as officer Gomes. Bob was amazed how easy that had been.

"Officer Gomes, I'm Bob Hillman. I was a close friend of Denise Crandall, a woman whose murder you investigated several months ago."

"Hello, Mr. Hillman. I'm sorry for your loss. I remember the case quite well. A rape and murder in Central Park with no suspects. What can I do for you?"

"Well, I wanted to mention something to you that's been haunting me ever since that tragedy and see if you think it casts some light on the case."

"Okay, Mr. Hillman, let's hear it."

"At the funeral, Denise's best friend, Chris Dinsmore, was not among the mourners. That alone was surprising, but after the funeral I was unable to contact her. She was a very responsible physician. When I called her place of work at Columbia's P&S Hospital, they too had been surprised by her absence and were unable to contact her. I can't get her absence out of my mind and wonder if it has any spillover to the Denise Crandall case. And in case you were wondering, no one's been able to contact her since that time—not her husband and not her family."

"Thanks for this heads-up Mr. Hillman. I agree it's worth some further thought on our part. Give me a week or so and I'll get back to you. I agree it's odd. I don't believe in coincidences either."

Bob felt a small measure of relief. At least he'd shared that information with someone who might be able to make sense of it.

CHAPTER TWO

Marge Cameron was putting the finishing touches on her makeup.

She could hear Mitch singing in the shower. Life was running smoothly for her and Mitch. He apparently had some extra cash and was happy to spend it on better accommodations where they could enjoy each other a few times each week. She was unsure if his wife, Brenda, was totally in the dark about these trysts, but Mitch didn't seem to be feeling any pressure from her. Maybe that new stream of cash was also keeping her content and unwilling to rock the boat.

Mitch came out of the shower and toweled off in front of Marge. She enjoyed seeing him naked. It was an intimacy that she needed since her status as the 'other woman' was not secure.

When Mitch had gently advised her to cool her interest in the project Denise was working on she had been surprised and angry. After all, worker attendance fell into her domain as head of Human Resources.

Mitch didn't want to discuss his advice in any detail, but he made it clear that she should just do as he said in this instance. She didn't want to jeopardize their outside relationship so she gave in to him. It was only a few days later that Denise was dead and Mitch was moving the chemical process related to the low absenteeism group to another site in the plant.

Since that time their relationship had intensified and she was determined not to make any waves. She just "dumbed herself down,"

and the two of them seemed happier than ever.

With the dispersal of workers who exhibited the inexplicable superior attendance to other parts of the factory, the figures on worker absenteeism began to normalize. The attendance issue was now moot, although an explanation for the previous experience was lacking.

CHAPTER THREE

Lieutenant Gomes decided to quietly reopen the Crandall murder case, this time with a possible connection to the Chris Dinsmore disappearance. Eric Dinsmore, her husband, had called the police after there was no word from Christine for two days. The police had nothing to go on. Now though, viewed in light of the Crandall murder, they re-questioned her husband.

He indicated that the two women were fast friends and frequently lunched together in Central Park. As best he could recall they even had met in the park just days before the murder. Chris's disappearance was totally unexpected and made no sense to Eric. None of her possessions were missing and no one at work or in her circle of friends and family had any idea why *she* was missing.

Leslie called Lieutenant Gomes, doing routine follow-up on the Crandall unsolved murder that she'd covered. Gomes informed her that the murder was now tied to the disappearance of a physician, making the initial interpretation of a simple rape/murder less tenable. That was all the information Gomes was willing to impart. For Leslie it was a gift.

Bob had returned from San Francisco and was eager to help in the investigation. Although Gomes was uneasy about citizen assistance, she welcomed any additional information or insights he could offer. He had, after all, been responsible for her reopening the case.

He told Gomes about the project Denise was working on. Bob suggested they recover her computer and see what, if any, light it might shed on the investigation. Gomes told him that the computer had been missing from the victim's apartment just hours after the body was discovered.

Gomes thought back to the morning they had taken the body to the morgue. She recalled that the homicide team didn't find a key to her apartment anywhere on or near the body. Nor did they find one in her locked apartment. She was puzzled by the missing key, but now, with an interest in the computer, it took on added significance.

Gomes's call to the Crandall home was answered by Elaine Crandall. Gomes explained that the police had new information that renewed interest in the case. Elaine told her that Denise's possessions in the apartment had been moved to her parent's home and were stored in the basement. When Gomes inquired about the computer, Elaine confirmed that her daughter's computer had not been found in the apartment. Gomes assumed it had been stolen since no key to the apartment had been found.

Denise's mother's information confirmed that it hadn't been removed by the victim or her family for storage at her family's home for some personal reason before she was killed.

Gomes shared this information with Bob. The obvious guess was that someone used the missing key to take the computer. Why that was the only item taken was a mystery, but also a clue. Its content must have had special significance. A used, several years old laptop computer was hardly worth the risk to a stranger being seen entering or leaving the apartment.

A clue, but a clue to what? If the computer's content was important to the killer that didn't necessitate a well-disguised murder. There were less risky ways to get at the computer. Gomes left the Crandall murder file on her desk as a reminder to discuss the case with the head of her homicide division.

CHAPTER FOUR

Manny and Mitch were enjoying lunch at a popular Bronx Greek restaurant. They did this once every other week. It was Manny's way of debriefing Mitch now that he was a member of the "family."

"Manny, it's been smooth sailing the past few months. The product manufacture has been successfully moved to a site with good ventilation and a new team of workers has settled in just fine. I hope you're satisfied and feel the money you're paying me is buying you and your boss peace of mind."

"We're very satisfied, Mitch. You've proven your value so don't feel that you're still on trial. Relax, enjoy the dough and that fine looking woman you're spending afternoons with."

"It's reassuring to hear you say that, Manny."

"Your advice to take that student's computer was very well-received. The boss likes attention to details and that was one we were about to overlook. I assume you destroyed those reports she turned in as well. The police don't have anything to work with. That's why they're so quiet. Let's drink to a job well done."

CHAPTER FIVE

The only content on the computer that had any information other than mundane school matters and personal contacts had to be related to her project at Sampson. That was Bob's surmise. In the weeks that he and Denise had spent most of their waking hours together, her project was the only thing of special significance she'd been working on. They'd discussed it quite often but Bob had to admit he wasn't familiar with all aspects of her work. He did know that Mitchell Trent was her primary contact at Sampson and she'd given him one or two progress reports. Absent her computer he'd be a potential source to offer some insight regarding where her investigation had led her. He discussed this with Lieutenant Gomes and she agreed a visit to Trent was worthwhile.

"Lieutenant Gomes and Mr. Hillman to see you, Mr. Trent," Mitch's secretary announced. He came out of his office to greet the visitors and welcome them inside. They had made an appointment to see him the day before so this was no surprise. They, however, had offered little information about the reason for the visit. Mitch was a little on edge but managed to keep his unease under wraps.

"Coffee for either of you folks?"

Gomes answered for herself and turned to Bob, who nodded a yes.

"Two coffees, Melanie. No, make that three. I'm ready for a re-fill."

"We won't take much of your time, Mr. Trent. Mr. Hillman was a close friend of Denise Crandall. He brought some information to my attention that kindled new interest in the Crandall murder. I can't share that information with you, but suffice it to say, it raised some interest in Denise Crandall's recent activities involving Sampson. That's the reason we're sitting in your office today."

"I'll help you any way I can, Lieutenant, so ask away."

Gomes began the inquiry. "I understand she was doing some research here related to the unusual finding of improved attendance here in the plant."

"Quite true. I was mentoring her in that project. It was to be material for an honors paper in business school. She reported to me on two occasions, keeping me up to date on her findings. All I can say is that her research was very preliminary and offered no new insight into that unusual finding. That's about it."

Gomes continued the questioning. "Thank you, Mr. Trent. That's helpful. Mr. Hillman told me she was preparing an updated report for you. Did she turn in such a report? None was found in her room and her computer is missing."

"As I said, her results were very preliminary and were scheduled to be updated at our next meeting. She gave me a brief report and it contained nothing of importance. I didn't save it since I knew she was going to update it at our next session."

"Do you remember any of the content? That might be helpful."

"I believe she was planning on interviewing some of the workers, but there were no details regarding those contacts in her initial report."

Bob stepped in here and continued the questioning. "Mr. Trent, Denise told me she was on to something but didn't say what. My impression is that she felt it was of some significance and was more than the 'nothing of importance' you said was contained in the report she'd given you."

"Maybe that was going to be included in the next report, Mr. Hillman. I'm sorry the computer is gone. It may have contained that report."

Lieutenant Gomes rose and indicated the meeting was over.

"Thanks for your time Mr. Trent. We may be back if anything new comes up regarding Denise's research."

Mitch walked them out to the front entrance of Sampson.

As they drove away, Bob commented on the lack of any new findings. "I'm not sure I buy Trent's 'nothing of importance.' If her findings were not kind to Sampson he might have reason to downplay them. In any event, it seems we're no closer to learning what Denise uncovered in her research.

"I think I'll interview some of the workers she planned to visit. Maybe that way I can reconstruct that report Trent said he never received."

"Good thought, Bob. Keep me in the loop. Seems like we're still a long way from finding out what Denise was on to. I don't think my boss is going to let me spend a lot of hours on this case until there's good reason to believe we have a solid lead. I'm afraid at this point you'll have to fly on your own."

CHAPTER SIX

Elaine was a sophomore at Barnard when she met Larry Crandall. Her major at Barnard was English with an emphasis on early twentieth century American literature. Her intention was to teach in high school. He was a junior in the pharmacy school at Columbia. Larry was five years older than Elaine since he had completed a four-year undergraduate major in chemistry before entering pharmacy school.

Their first date was anything but a success. She was a buoyant, vivacious young woman and he was a quiet, somewhat dour guy with a nerdy wardrobe. They certainly were an odd couple, as Elaine's friends were quick to point out. Nevertheless they continued to date. She enjoyed his acid sense of humor. She also admired his very sober take on things and events around them. She saw him as far more aggressive than her friends imagined. He was not destined to spend his life behind a pharmacy counter, filling prescriptions and selling a host of retail products that had nothing to do with pharmacy. No, he was destined for something bigger and better than most pharmacy graduates imagined for themselves.

Larry and Elaine were quite compatible while in school and married six months before she graduated. The birth of Denise soon after graduation put her work plans on hold and she never got back on track. Another child, their son Alex, came just a year later and Elaine's life as mother and homemaker was now cast in concrete. Strangely enough, she didn't long for the life not pursued and Larry didn't push her in that direction.

Larry and Mitch Trent were building a chemical company that was still in the break-even stage. Larry headed the company, and worked with great zeal. Work began to dominate his life and his marriage became secondary. Elaine accepted her modest life style and role as a stay-at-home mom. Her relationship with Larry began to slowly wither. He tended to work late, travel a lot, and have little interest in the leisure activities she wanted to pursue. She had plenty of time to search out such activities but he became reclusive and emotionally remote. She knew little about his work and had little interest in it. Aside from their children they led separate lives.

Elaine's brief fling with an old friend from college days started off with a lot of heat, but his family obligations proved too weighty for him to sustain it. She got out unscathed after a year without Larry knowing about the affair. She wondered if he would have cared. Larry was an enigma to her.

Larry had no friends and even kept Mitch at a distance. In private he did have one form of enjoyment and that was proving how clever he could be. No one else need know. This was for internal consumption, something he only had to prove to himself to be satisfied.

The death of Denise had hit him hard but he had no inkling that he was indirectly responsible for her death. Oscar's planned elimination of two women was not brought to his attention. Oscar didn't even know that one of the women was Larry's daughter. He never asked Manny what their names were.

There were no other women in Larry's life aside from Elaine. She had become increasingly social and high-spirited as their children aged out of the house. For Larry, her metamorphosis made them less compatible. He didn't care for her upbeat style of life and only went along with it to maintain the appearance of a loving married couple. Keeping up with Elaine was the major challenge in his life.

CHAPTER SEVEN

Bob was perplexed. Mitch Trent, Denise's company mentor, seemingly knew next to nothing about the issue she'd been investigating. That was strange. Her printed reports had been trashed by Mitch and her computer was conveniently missing. Denise was unable to speak for herself. Her closest friend, whom she would have confided in, was missing. Moreover, the unexplained low absenteeism no longer existed at Sampson. It was as if Denise and her project never existed. The one incontrovertible fact was that Denise had been murdered. Was this related to the now perfectly clean slate at Sampson or was it just a brutal homicide with no connection? And what about her missing friend? He couldn't let it go. Something was amiss but he had nothing to work with. He was meeting Elaine for lunch and would quiz her gently about Sampson and its management.

Elaine drove into Manhattan and met Bob at a classy, white tablecloth Italian restaurant on the Upper East Side.

Bob arrived first and was there to greet Elaine when she made her entrance. He couldn't help but recall his first meeting with Denise at Barney Greengrass. Elaine was Denise plus twenty years. She was vibrant, smiling, and very appealing. Their table was ready so they sat down and ordered wine.

After some light banter, Bob asked Elaine to tell him what she knew about Denise's project.

"I don't know a lot. I first became aware of the job attendance issue when Marge Cameron, a good friend and the HR person at Sampson, told me about it. When I told her Denise was looking for a topic for her senior paper, she agreed to help Denise. That's how it all got started."

Bob saw this as a lead to follow up. Surely the HR officer would be looking into this matter.

"That's about all I can tell you. Denise and I never had an opportunity to delve into her findings."

"What about your friend, the HR officer, did she ever discuss it with you?"

"Nope. It never came up again after she brought it to my attention."

Elaine was curious why Bob was taking this interest in Denise's research project. She found it painful to talk about her daughter and wanted to steer the conversation elsewhere.

"Bob, why this interest in Denise's project? We were both hurt in the extreme by her death, so why go over this painful past history? I want to push it as far back in my memory as possible, not keep it in front of me to continue grieving."

"I share that feeling, Elaine, but I have reason to doubt that her death was a random event. I've given the police a reason to reopen the case and I'm helping them pursue a new approach to the murder. Forgive me for inflicting pain on you. I just can't let it rest as long as I sense that there's more behind her death than was apparent at first."

Elaine grew silent and Bob gave her a moment to decide whether to proceed any further. She looked him directly in the eye and gave him a brave smile. Her eyes, which had begun to tear up earlier, were now dry.

"Okay. I want to do whatever is necessary to help find the truth about what happened to my daughter. Tell me about the new information that has reopened the case."

Bob gave Elaine an update, sharing with her the information he imparted to the police. She absorbed it in resolute silence.

CHAPTER EIGHT

N ow that Leslie was convinced that the murder of Denise Crandall was not a simple rape/murder she needed to learn how the disappearance of a physician had prompted the police to reopen the case.

She discussed her options with Chan. "How can I get the name of the missing physician, Chan? Can you help me?"

"Sure, Leslie, I'll contact NYPD Missing Persons and search for a missing person who also happens to be a physician. I'll target my search to the days surrounding the Crandall murder. I should turn up something useful. I don't think a lot of doctors go missing."

"Great, Chan. I'm sure this is a critical lead for me."

The next day, Leslie got the name from Chan.

"Christine Dinsmore M.D. is the physician you want to investigate. Police records list her as a neurologist at Columbia Presbyterian.
She's married and thirty-eight years old. The preliminary investigation
has yielded nothing. Her husband, Eric Dinsmore, reported her missing
and so far there are no leads whatsoever. His cellphone number is given
as 212-453-7762."

"You're incredible, Chan. I'm off and running."

Eric Dinsmore didn't recognize the name when his phone began
ringing. He was sitting in his office staring out the window at the Hudson
River and New Jersey. Since Chris's disappearance he did a lot of staring
into the distance. The ringing broke the trance and he decided to answer
the call.

"This is Eric. How can I help you?"

"Thanks for taking my call Mr. Dinsmore. I'm Leslie Nugent, a
reporter with *The Times*. Do you have a minute? I'm writing a follow-up
article on the Denise Crandall murder and your wife Chris's name has
come into the picture. It would be really helpful if I could meet with you
and learn why her disappearance has prompted the police to reopen the
Crandall murder investigation."

"Okay, Ms. Nugent. I want to help any way I can. I'll do anything
that may shed some light on Chris's disappearance. I can meet you for
drinks today about three o'clock at the Darby Grill on Third Avenue and
28th Street."

"Fantastic, Mr. Dinsmore. I'll see you there. I'm wearing a black
and white striped slipover top and have long, straight blond hair."

The Darby Grill was a short Uber ride from Leslie's office at *The
Times*. She arrived before Eric and was seated. She gave the maître d' her
name, so Eric had no trouble getting to her table.

"I'm Eric Dinsmore, Ms. Nugent. Nice to meet you."

"Thanks again for meeting with me, Mr. Dinsmore."

"Please, Ms. Nugent, let's use first names. I'm Eric and you're Leslie. Okay?"

He took a seat opposite and they immediately jumped to the matter at hand. "I'm looking for a connection between your wife and the Crandall woman. There must be something."

"Well, that's an easy one to answer. They were best friends and Chris disappeared on the same day that Denise was murdered in the park. Quite a coincidence, isn't it?"

"I'd say so. Can you think of any possible circumstance tying them together other than close friendship, Eric?"

"Chris is a neurologist at Columbia and Denise was an MBA student at Columbia. That's hardly a connection of any significance. Denise had a close friend named Bob Hillman who could probably fill you in on what Denise was up to, if anything, aside from her schoolwork. All I can tell you about Chris is that she works very hard in her practice and also supervises a neurology clinic at Presbyterian Hospital. My guess is that Denise had something going that dovetailed with Chris's neurology work. I can't imagine a connection in any other direction."

"That's a start, Eric. Knowing that they were close friends is a help."

"I understand that Hillman's a major player in the energy field, so I bet if you Google him, you're likely to come up with a way to reach him. That would be my next step. He might offer some help with the question you're asking. I wish I could be more helpful."

"I've already met him, Eric. I did an interview with him for an article in *The Times*."

Leslie smiled and shook her head in agreement.

"You've been a big help, Eric."

CHAPTER NINE

Bob chose to meet with Marjorie Cameron off the Sampson campus. His call to her office was met with a cheery voice and a willingness to talk about the Sampson attendance issue. Her interest in the matter took him by surprise. It was almost as if she'd been waiting for such a call. They met at a restaurant upriver in Hastings, highly recommended in Zagat, Bob's restaurant bible for out-of-towners. It overlooked the Hudson and made good use of the view.

He arrived a bit late in his rental car, being unfamiliar with the roads in the area. Marge was already seated and had a glass of white wine in her hand as she rose to greet him. He was met by the charming smile of a very lovely woman whom he guessed to be in her late thirties or early forties.

"I'm very pleased to meet you Ms. Cameron. I appreciate your willingness to meet with me, a total stranger, to discuss your workplace."

"You use Marge, and I'll use Bob if that's okay with you."

Marge found herself shifting into a mildly flirtatious mode as she felt the undeniable attraction of a good looking male across the table from her.

"That's a good start, Marge. Why don't we study the menu and get ordering out of the way before we get serious?" They made their selections and Bob ordered a glass of Chardonnay for himself. She ordered a refill of her glass of wine.

"Before we start, let me tell you that I'm a businessman from San Francisco who was very close to Denise Crandall at the time of her death. I'm not satisfied that the police initially examined her life carefully enough to entertain alternate theories of her murder. That's what I'm doing. Having put my brief bio behind us, I'll tell you what little I know about you and Sampson in the context of the matter Denise Crandall was investigating."

"I didn't know you and Denise were involved with each other, Bob. We weren't that friendly and only knew each other briefly through her recent involvement at Sampson."

"Marge, I know that you're the HR person at Sampson, so I assume you were very into the absenteeism mystery that Denise was exploring for a paper she was going to write. I also know you're a close friend of Elaine Crandall and actually are the person who brought the matter to Elaine's attention, who then the passed it on to Denise. That's all just background. What can you tell me about the matter from the HR perspective?"

"When I tell you what I know you may wonder why we're having this lunch meeting that you graciously offered to pay for when you invited me. I know very little. I suspect Denise knew far more than me."

"That really surprises me. I'd have thought HR would have been all over the matter."

"Normally, we would be. In this instance my boss, Mitchell Trent, nudged me aside and seemed to take over my HR role in this matter. I don't know why he kept me away from it and kept Denise's output to himself. When I tried to work my way in, it was clear that he assigned me a benchwarmer's role. I took the not-so-subtle hint. And that's it."

"That's more than curious, Marge. Do you have any idea why he behaved in this manner?"

"None whatsoever."

"I was with Lieutenant Claudia Gomes from homicide when she questioned Mr. Trent. He claimed to have received no information of interest from Denise and had even trashed her initial report."

"That report was handed to me by Denise. Before I could read it, Mitch, I mean Mr. Trent, took it from my desk saying he wanted to read it first and would return it to me when he was through with it. He never did."

"So he froze you out and never brought you back into an area of your legitimate interest. Let me switch gears here. What can you tell me about Mr. Trent?"

"Mitch is a good friend and my boss, so I don't think I can offer you any deep info about him. That wouldn't be consistent with our relationship."

"Okay, Marge. That's fair. I respect the boundaries of your friendship."

Marge hated to bring her relationship with Mitch into the discussion.

"Oh, yes," offered Marge. "One more thing. Denise wanted to interview some of the men in the low absenteeism group. I gave her a list of their names and addresses. I don't know if she actually interviewed any of them."

"That list might be helpful. Could you give me a copy of it? Just email it to me at the address on this card."

"Shall do, Bob. You'll have it tomorrow."

CHAPTER TEN

L eslie met regularly with her editor, Clayton Garfield, at *the Times* to get guidance on stories she was working on. He had previously sent her on the Hillman interview. That had resulted in a quality story and earned Leslie some valuable points in his eyes.

As a new hire, her editor offered suggestions about items she was developing to determine if they had a high likelihood of making it into print. He was a checkpoint to keep her from spinning her wheels. The Crandall murder had offered the prospect of a big city crime story, but so far Leslie had not uncovered any hot new angles about the murder. She had unearthed the coincidental disappearance of Denise's close friend, but was yet to find the significance, if any, of that finding.

Leslie felt she was on the verge of something that would move the story ahead and justify keeping it alive on her work schedule. Her editor was less sanguine, but Leslie's presentation was strong and won her some more time to raise the story's reader appeal. He admired her determination but questioned her realistic expectation.

Today she was going to seek out one of Denise's teachers at the business school to flesh out the dead woman's recent life story. She was hoping something would jump out to help her understand why she was murdered.

The registrar at the business school was very helpful. She had read Leslie's piece in *The Times* and recognized the victim as one of her students. She told Leslie that Aaron Leibman had been Denise's advisor and would probably know more about her recent school activities than anyone else. She also alerted Leslie to the fact that Professor Leibman was about to retire and was spending his time these days packing up his office. She told her how to find his office and called ahead to alert the professor that a visitor was coming over.

Retirement was now a reality for Aaron Leibman. Forty years at Columbia had passed by in the blink of an eye. He had no regrets. His career in the law school and business school had been rewarding, both professionally and personally. Now it was time to empty out his office and make way for a new faculty person. This was the final moment, the one that put the final punctuation on his career.

He had packed up the books that mattered to him. His extensive library on contracts, accumulated over four decades, filled four large cartons. Few of the remaining books held any lasting interest to him. The few that did didn't even fill the remaining carton.

The last remains of his faculty life were in the file drawers of his desk. This was the tricky part. What was worth saving among the many file folders? This was a trip into the past as he quickly browsed each folder.

He was almost ready to break for lunch when he lifted out the folder labeled "Crandall project." A quick review of the slim content of the folder reminded him what it was about. His recall was acute. Denise

A.S. MOST

Crandall had asked him, as her faculty advisor, to provide guidance on the project she had chosen as the subject for her honor's paper. He recalled Denise as a bright and witty young woman who was older than the usual business school student. He enjoyed meeting with her.

Reading through the folder he saw that the project never was completed. *Why?* he asked himself. It was a good topic for an honor's paper. He started to read his notes in chronological order. He and Denise had met at least three or four times to discuss the project.

His notes told him that the unusual low absenteeism issue was sidelined when she discovered that two workers had developed similar neurological problems. They discussed this and concluded that she would tell a senior management person at Sampson and encourage a call to OSHA. His notes indicated that the Sampson COO had been helping her on the project and was the logical person to be given the information. Denise indicated that she would also tell her father since he was the company President. That was his last note in the file. He lay the folder down and leaned back in his leather desk chair.

So what happened? he pondered. It was like watching a tense drama on TV and having the power go out. It appeared that the project never was finished. In fact, he never saw Denise again. That was odd. He had anticipated at least one more follow-up visit. This had occurred during a busy time for him. His wife was entering the final stage of Alzheimer's and that had consumed much of his time and attention. He'd lost track of many other office responsibilities to wrap up.

Calling the phone number for Denise in his file told him the phone was no longer in service. He took that to mean she had moved after graduation. He next called the registrar to find her forwarding address and phone number. There wasn't any, only a number to call in case of emergency. He let it rest.

The review of files had taken place over the past week. It was difficult to accept that this phase of his life was over.

127

The knock on his door broke his reverie.

"Come in, it's not locked."

The person who entered was a young woman dressed casually in a sweater and skirt. She could easily pass for a student or young faculty member.

"You must be the visitor they called about. Come in, young lady, clear off a chair, and have a seat. I don't have many visitors these days. Tell me who you are and why you want to see a relic of a faculty member."

"Thanks for your warm welcome, Professor. I'm Leslie Nugent, a reporter with *The Times*, and I'm here to talk about Denise Crandall."

"That's a coincidence. I was thinking about Denise earlier this week and wondering whatever happened to the project we were working on. I was her faculty advisor. I tried to reach her to find out what happened to her honor's project I was advising her on. My last notes said she was pursuing an unexpected finding that came up in the project. I'm retiring and was going over some of my folders. I came across one with notes on my meetings with Denise."

"Let me stop you, Professor Leibman. I guess you don't know that Denise is dead. She never graduated. She was murdered in Central Park. That's why her project was never completed."

Aaron was speechless. He sat with his eyes closed for a long moment. When they opened they were filled with tears. "I'm stunned. She was a wonderful student to work with. I take this as a very real personal loss. I'm heartbroken for her and her family."

A silence came over them as they each processed the loss.

"Professor, would you be so kind as to let me read those notes you have? They're probably among the last reflections on her life. She died very soon after that last meeting with you. I'm hoping to write a series of stories on the murder and I'm looking for any clue that would explain her murder. The police have good reason to believe it was not a random act of violence."

"I'm still having trouble imagining her dead, Ms. Nugent. She was vibrant and so enthusiastic about her work. I can't recall a more promising student."

After a pause, he continued. "Of course you can see the notes. In fact I'm giving them to you. Maybe they'll help you unravel the mystery of this terrible loss." With that, he handed her the folder that was lying on top of a pile of others on his desk.

"They're handwritten but I think they're legible. Let me summarize what Denise had found. I was reviewing the notes just before you came to my office. Her original study, focused on the low absenteeism, was sidelined by the finding of a possibly toxic workplace at Sampson and the need to bring this to the attention of the COO so he could contact OSHA. That's the gist."

"Is there anything else you can tell me, Professor Leibman?"

"Not at this moment, Ms. Nugent. I'm still just shocked."

"Thanks again for your time and for these notes. May I keep them or do you want them back?"

"You can keep them. I hope they help you."

"I'll call you if I may, should any questions arise as I process the information in your notes."

"Certainly, Ms. Nugent. Here's my cellphone number." He wrote down the number and handed the piece of paper to her. "I'm so glad you came by. I was going to say it was a pleasure to meet you but that seems out of place, given the context."

"It looks like you're winding up a long and fruitful career here at Columbia. You must have many good memories of your time here. I wish you well in the next phase of your life."

Leslie shook his hand and left. She couldn't wait to sit down and read the notes. She also now planned on visiting Sampson and finding out if OSHA was ever called.

CHAPTER ELEVEN

After hearing what Mitch reported about his meeting with the homicide lieutenant, Manny stopped in to see Oscar.

The office was dimly lit by a floor lamp in one corner and a desk lamp with one sixty-watt bulb. It was characteristically neat; not unused, just well-ordered in spite of the considerable amount of paper material on various tables, cabinet tops, and the large mahogany desk. Oscar kept a bottle of Jameson scotch and two glasses on the credenza behind him. It was mostly for show since he rarely drank hard liquor, and then, only to be sociable.

In his usual understated manner, Oscar had a fix on the situation. "I want to hear what you make of this, Manny."

"Well, I think it's worth keeping an eye on the man who accompanied the detective. He was introduced to Mitch as a close friend of the woman killed in the park so he might be specially motivated to pursue his own investigation if the police back off. I wouldn't want there to be any more people events at this time that could stimulate greater interest on the part of the police. If they begin to put the pieces together I wouldn't want to give them more pieces to play with."

"Very good, Manny. Is that a picture puzzle you were alluding to? Anyway, I agree that anymore killing at this point would throw another log on a dying fire. Let's maintain our cool and encourage Mitch to be vigilant. Is that enough of a plan, Manny?"

"A very good one at that, Oscar. And I like your dying fire metaphor. You know, maybe we're too high-toned for this business."

CHAPTER TWELVE

M itch's secretary put down her nail file and invited the young woman into her office.

"How can I help you, Miss?" was her cheery welcome to Leslie.

"I'm Leslie Nugent, a reporter from *The New York Times*. I'm looking for Mr. Trent, your COO. The sign outside says I'm in the right place. I called earlier and was told he'd be in and available at this time. I probably spoke to you."

"Yes, you did. He just stepped out for an unscheduled meeting but will be back in less than half an hour. It shouldn't be a long meeting. Perhaps you'd like to talk to Marge Cameron, our HR officer. Her office is just down the hall and I think she's free." She pointed a long, well-shaped nail in the direction of the office.

"Sounds like a good idea. I'll just wander over there and knock on her door, if that's okay?"

"Sure. We don't stand on ceremony here. Why don't you head over there and I'll phone ahead to let her know you're coming?"

"Thanks. You've been very kind."

Leslie turned, left the office, and headed down the hall to the office of Marjorie Cameron.

Marge greeted her in the doorway and invited her in.

"We don't see many reporters here and certainly not one from *The Times*. I'm curious to know what you're looking for. Have a seat and tell me how I can be of help. Mr. Trent may be awhile. And please, call me Marge and I'll call you Leslie."

"Well, Marge, it has to do with the murder of Denise Crandall. I'm doing a series on her death. Information I recently obtained led me here. As head of HR, you probably are well aware of two employees who have recently developed similar neurological problems, possibly indicating a toxin in their work environment."

Marge looked surprised. "This may come as a shock to you, Leslie, but I'm not aware of that problem. What does this have to do with Denise? I know she was doing a study relating to our low absenteeism but that was all I knew. Mr. Trent was her principal contact here and he was the only person privy to her reports. It's funny you should be inquiring about Denise's study since a gentleman was in here just the other day with a similar interest. I gave him a list of names of the workers Denise interviewed. He was 'shadowing' her, trying to find any clue as to why she was murdered. I'd be happy to give you the same list, if that would be of any help to you."

"Thank you, Marge. That would be helpful. I'm curious. Who was this gentleman you mentioned?"

"Guy's name is Bob Hillman. He was a close friend of Denise's. He didn't leave a phone number but I bet Denise's mother might have it."

"That's okay, Marge, I think I have a number for him."

"I'm going to print out the list for you now." She typed on her computer keyboard and her printer delivered a list of names and phone numbers. Marge handed the paper to Leslie.

"You're great Marge. I just have one more question. Was there an OSHA investigation here to follow up the question of a toxic work environment?"

"None that I'm aware of, Leslie, and I'd certainly know if there was one."

With that, Leslie rose to leave. "I think that winds up my visit here. There's no need for me to talk to Mr. Trent at this time. Here's my card if you think of anything I ought to know about Sampson pertaining to Denise. Thanks, again, Marge."

Leslie left. She was glad Trent was late so she could avoid seeing him. She hoped to avoid him until she felt the moment was ripe to ask him why OSHA had never been called. She also was interested to speak to Bob Hillman and find out what his interviews had told him.

CHAPTER THIRTEEN

The first three interviewees on Bob's list recalled meeting Denise and remembered her as charming and easy to talk to. Bob's sessions were unrewarding. On the third interview it was apparent that the man's leg problem was making it difficult for him to work. He told Bob that Denise had been interested in his problem and that his wife had told her that a co-worker, James Healy, had a similar problem.

Mrs. Tyler had been listening from the adjoining kitchen and now came into the room.

"Ethan may not remember, but I told the young woman that the Healy's had visited a doctor and had his legs examined. Virginia Healy recommended that we see the same doctor and gave me the doctor's business card. When I called to make an appointment the clinic secretary told me that doctor was not available and referred me to another physician. I told her a friend had recommended us to Dr. Dinsmore and that we would wait for a later appointment, but she told us Dr. Dinsmore was just not available."

Bob felt a chill run down his back. He was stunned and unable to speak for a moment.

Mrs. Tyler voiced her concern. "Are you okay, Mr. Hillman? You look kinda pale. Would you like some water?"

Bob recovered and tried to tie down the information Denise had uncovered.

"Did she have any comment when you told her about the doctor you were trying to see?"

"Well, no. As a matter of fact she rather quickly ended our interview and seemed to be in a hurry to leave. She was polite, but the information appeared to change her mood. She became very serious. The change was remarkable, all due to some information about that doctor."

"Let me get back to your foot problem, Mr. Tyler. Has it changed in the past few weeks since you were moved to a new worksite?" "Not really. I'd say there was no change either way. If you see Jim, he'll probably tell you much the same thing. We were both moved to a new worksite along with our entire crew. We're now working on a new product."

Bob rose to leave and thanked the Tylers. Outside, sitting in his car, his mind was running a mile a minute. He now saw a connection between Denise's death and Chris's disappearance. They each had a common experience: Sampson workers with similar nerve problems. But how does this have anything to do with a murder and disappearance? He couldn't make that connection, if there was one. But there had to be some connection. Now, more than ever, he had to pursue the mystery to completion.

CHAPTER FOURTEEN

Bob had only met Eric Dinsmore once, at a party where he was introduced to Eric and Chris by Denise. The two men hit it off and found themselves agreeing on most things political and social. Eric was in a solo, private law practice mainly focused on serving the varied needs of a high profile client. Without saying as much, Bob surmised that he was a "fixer" for this client, prized for his confidentiality and willingness to shoulder less savory tasks. He was well paid for his grey zone exploits. In spite of this somewhat seamy aspect of his practice, Bob and Eric found themselves bound together by their common losses.

Eric had the highest praise for Denise and had let Bob know what a lucky guy he'd been. Now they were two lonely guys having dinner at a quiet midtown Manhattan steakhouse. Their once happy twosomes had abruptly been reduced to singles. Although Eric held out the fading hope that Chris was going to turn up someday, he readily admitted that the signs pointed to her being gone with finality. He was a widower with no grave to mourn at.

"Hard to believe what's happened to us in such a short time, Bob."

"I'm weighed down by my grief too, Eric, but I'm also intent on solving the mystery surrounding our loss. That's why I wanted to see you. I have information that says it's no coincidence that the two women met untimely ends so close together in time. When you hear what I've uncovered, I hope you'll share my determination to dig around and find the reason for our losses."

In the next ten minutes, Bob explained to Eric how Denise, in her interviews of Sampson workers, had chanced on one with a nerve problem in his feet.

"That man had a co-worker with a very similar problem. Chris was seeing that other worker as a patient in her clinic. This established that the two women were privy to information probably unknown to others. The HR person at Sampson had been unaware of the information. Just what the COO, Mitch Trent, knew was unclear since Denise's report or reports to him were unavailable, though he denied any important finding on her part. Undoubtedly, the women shared their information between them."

Bob paused. He felt he was rushing to get all the information out that he'd gathered just a few days ago. He started again, but slower this time.

"One other small detail: the nerve problem had developed since the men began working on a new product line. To me, and certainly Denise, it suggests that the new product may have created a toxic situation in the work area of the two men. Furthermore, the crew working on the new product has since been moved to another worksite and is working on a different product."

"I follow you, Bob, but how does that information tie into Denise being murdered in the park and Chris vanishing?"

"The way I see it, we have two women sharing information they were not supposed to have, and then we have the two of them being abruptly removed from the picture. There has to be some linkage here. I can feel it. Someone believed the information was a threat to their interest. What can *you* make of it, Eric?"

"I see where you're coming from, Bob, but the findings could all be unrelated. The men with nerve problems could be related to a toxic atmosphere at work and Denise's killing and Chris's disappearance could be unrelated. In either event, was the finding of a toxic environment sufficient reason for what happened to the two women?"

"That's all we've got. Now I need your help to see if we can take this conjecture further. I say 'we' because two guys are less conspicuous sniffing around than one guy. I know you're an attorney so you would add a useful skillset to our team of two. I'm just a businessman with deep pockets. Well, I also had two tours with the marines in Afghanistan, but I'm no Green Beret in the John Wayne mode. I only mention this because there could be an element of danger in this work. Two people are dead. I think what's being concealed must be worth a great deal to justify the elimination of two relative innocents. Can I count you in?"

Eric turned grim as he contemplated what lay ahead. Then, abruptly, he brightened up and gave Bob an affirmative thumbs up. "I'm all for it, Bob. I owe it to Chris."

"Great. Let's meet tomorrow and put together a strategic plan."

Bob left and Eric stayed behind to gather his thoughts. He now saw the small drug operation in Yonkers that Alyssa had set up with little help from him was possibly involved, somehow, in Chris's disappearance. It had been left off the radar screen because it was a minor operation. Now it was coming into view and he didn't like what he saw.

CHAPTER FIFTEEN

The low man on the totem pole wasn't fed great stories by his or her editor. Leslie had to dig for stories and her fellow reporters were out digging in the same turf. One advantage she had was her relationship with Chan Young. The relationship was genuine. In no way was she using Chan as a news source in a pejorative sense. Back in D.C. she'd had a "lover" who fed her valuable tidbits of insider gossip. That relationship had ended badly and never reached the level of true friendship she felt with Chan. On the other hand, Chan understood her need for leads and was happy to help wherever he could, within the confines of department rules regarding confidentiality. Sometimes the guidelines were fuzzy so he had to be wary.

Tonight they were enjoying some weed in Leslie's apartment. They enjoyed the freedom of the apartment. Her time with Chan was relaxing.

Leslie felt that Chan was a guy she could be intimate with, but was not willing to deceive him. They were good friends and she believed sexual contact would alter their friendship. She didn't want a romantic relationship so she unilaterally declared it out-of-bounds.

"Chan, I think we need to be upfront about our feelings. This setting is conducive to intimate contact and I don't want to start down that road. I need to know that you understand that. I value your friendship."

Chan was silent for a moment as he thought about his response.

"Leslie, our friendship is solid. I don't want to add a layer of complexity. Let's agree that we're good friends and let it go at that."

"Chan, I feel better knowing that we're in agreement on that.

Chan's stories were good leads and some had matured into very powerful human interest tales. Leslie's editor was pleased with her story production and talked about moving her up on the ladder for better story material.

CHAPTER SIXTEEN

Her call to Bob Hillman's number was answered promptly.

"Hello, you've reached Bob Hillman. Your name is familiar but I can't place it in any context."

"So much for the impression I made on you, Mr. Hillman. I'm Leslie Nugent, the *Times* reporter who interviewed you a number of weeks ago."

"Ah, yes. Now I remember. I was going to call your paper and thank them for sending over their most attractive reporter. I forgot to do that but it's never too late." He paused a moment but quickly became serious. "Sorry for that diversion, Ms. Nugent. What can I do for you?"

"Nothing so lighthearted, Bob. You did let us operate on a first name basis before so I'm assuming that rule still applies."

"Of course, Leslie. What's on your mind?"

"I think we have a common interest, the murder of Denise Crandall. I have information that might interest you and you may have some for me. We should probably get together and do some sharing."

"I remember the interview now, Leslie. Your article was very objective and made the points I hoped to get across. About the murder, I agree that we should exchange information. I'm eager for any help that may make sense of the murder of an innocent business school student, and a missing neurologist at Columbia."

Leslie was pleased that he was so receptive. Their interview had gone so well. Maybe even better than that. She had found him very engaging and wondered how he had sized her up. He'd been involved with Denise at the time. That probably explained the absence of any follow-up call.

Life is full of surprises, she thought.

"You name a spot and I'll be there, Bob."

"Okay, Leslie. I'm game. Let's do it. How about dinner tonight at Molyvos on Seventh Avenue?"

"Can do. Pick a time."

"I'll call for a reservation at eight. Assume that's done."

"That's fine. I'll be wearing a navy skirt and a blue and white striped blouse under a light grey cardigan."

"I remember you very well. I don't think I'll have trouble recognizing you. See you at eight."

Bob hung up and had a funny sensation. The conversation was reminiscent of the first time he had called Denise. Very friendly and even inviting. For the first time in a while he was looking forward to going out to dinner.

Five hours later Bob arrived at Molyvos and was escorted to a quiet corner table by the maître d'. He had chosen Molyvos for its quiet, confident manner. A good place for conversation and a very good place if you liked Greek food. He recalled Leslie from the interview. If circumstances had been different, he might have pursued her.

The woman approaching his table was slim, thirty-five-ish or so with straight dirty blond hair and head-turning good looks. He rose to greet her.

"You picked a great place for dinner, Bob. I love Greek food."

"I had you figured for an octopus lover, and who does octopus better than the Greeks? I'm glad you liked my choice."

Leslie settled into the seat opposite Bob and gave him a friendly smile.

Leslie saw a tall, well-tanned man with an athletic build. His black hair with flecks of grey was a bit long for a New Yorker and was loosely combed. Not a New Yorker by his clothing, either. Since she had interviewed him, she knew she was facing a very successful businessman from the far west. She actually knew quite a bit about him before the interview and the interview itself had just deepened her knowledge. He had Googled her before dinner but gleaned very little from a short terse bio piece. It confirmed her *Times* credentials and referred to a big story she'd written as a special for *The Washington Post*, but offered little more.

"I know a lot about you, Bob, but I suspect you don't know much about me. Let me fill you in. I'm not new to New York. I was born here. I came back from D.C. where I worked on a small paper in northern Virginia for nearly ten years. I wrote a big story on the president's illness for *The Washington Post*. You may have seen it, and that brought me to *The Times* about a year ago. I covered the rape/murder of Denise Crandall in its first iteration and my editor has allowed me to write some follow-up pieces if I can uncover any new and interesting information. I think I have and that brings you up to date."

"Sounds like an upward trajectory, Leslie."

"I guess so, but I'm just a junior reporter after more than a decade in the game. I shouldn't complain and I'm not."

"Let's order, Leslie, and then get down to business."

"Think I'll pass on the octopus, if you don't mind, Bob. I know you meant well. I'm game for any fish without tentacles or suckers."

"Treat's on me, Leslie, so don't let the lobster prices scare you off."

"I read your bio so I figured this was gonna be a free meal for me. My salary versus yours has got to be a grotesque mismatch."

Bob was having déjà vu. This was like Denise reincarnated and meeting him at Barney Greengrass. The waiter came by and took their drink and food order.

"Now let's see what we have to trade, Leslie. Let me go first. I alerted the police to the absence of Chris Dinsmore at Denise's funeral and the fact that her best friend, Chris, went missing on the same day Denise was killed. They confirmed this and decided that the coincidence was enough to reopen their investigation and consider Denise's death other than a simple rape/murder. You probably don't know about this because you haven't written about it in a follow-up article."

"Not so fast, Bob. Lieutenant Gomes did clue me in to the fact that Denise's death was now coupled with the disappearance of a physician. I was able to obtain the identity of that missing person: a doctor Dinsmore. Her husband confirmed the close friendship between the two women."

"So, Leslie, we're even on that score. Next, I interviewed the same people at Sampson that Denise did as part of her senior project. I found that Denise and Chris shared information about two Sampson workers suffering from similar problems in their feet. Now don't tell me you've uncovered the same information. As far as I know, no one knows about this."

"Sorry to disappoint you again, Bob. I spoke with Aaron Leibman, a professor in the business school. He was Denise's advisor on her senior project. He gave me his notes from meetings with her and they make clear that Denise recognized a toxic workplace was the likely cause of the problem the two workers had with their feet."

"Fascinating. Once again, we arrive at the same juncture but by different routes. I find that amazing, Leslie."

"So much for your fascination, Bob. The question is, what does a murder and a mysterious disappearance have to do with this? It seems that the two women shared some medical information that proved fatal to them both."

"If it was just medical information, Leslie, it wouldn't have proven fatal. The information must have significance that goes beyond medicine."

"I agree, Bob. I do have one other piece of information. Professor Leibman's notes indicate that Denise was going to bring this toxicity issue to the Sampson COO and expected that he would contact OSHA. I met Marge Cameron, the HR head at Sampson, and she was unaware of any OSHA investigation at Sampson. What does that say? Is there a cover-up here?"

"That's very interesting, Leslie. It again suggests this is not a simple case of a toxic work environment. We need to wring more significance out of the facts we've uncovered. But maybe do that after our meal is consumed. It looks like it's heading our way now."

The conversation turned more personal as they dug into their food. The case discussion had made them ravenous. As their empty plates were being removed, Bob took a chance and asked Leslie if she'd like to have dessert at a nearby coffee house specializing in French pastries. She was agreeable and the two of them went off together, each harboring thoughts about the other that were neither case-related nor reflective of just a two-hour dinner.

CHAPTER SEVENTEEN

Eric was in a bind. From what Bob had learned and shared with him, Denise and Chris had innocently stumbled on a toxic environment at Sampson. Their appropriate response had been to advise Sampson to call in OSHA. That, of course, would put the Sampson-York combine out of business and under the gun of the DEA once the nature of the chemicals being processed was defined. It was unclear how far the government's reach would extend. His job was to keep Alyssa informed and limit any damage that could result.

Bob Hillman was pushing this matter forward, so staying in close contact with him was one way to monitor his progress before he caused any damage. Playing the turncoat partner was a role he didn't relish, but it seemed the best way to keep tabs on what Bob found out and was planning.

Alyssa would hear him out and decide if this was the best course of action. He needed her OK if he was to carry out this subterfuge.

"I didn't expect to see you again so soon, Eric. I've just heard that your wife is now officially a missing person. You have my sincerest concern, Eric. If I can be of any help please let me be involved. I met Christine on several occasions and found her to be a warm and sincere person."

"I appreciate that, Alyssa. I miss her terribly. I'm trying to remain optimistic that she'll return unharmed, but we both know the odds don't favor a good outcome."

His eyes misted over and Alyssa came out from behind her desk and embraced him. They were silent for a moment and then separated.

"You didn't come in here for my sympathy. What's on your mind?"

"Remember that little 'hiccup' we discussed a few weeks ago? It involved the Sampson-York combine. There was a vague threat that the drug operation might be uncovered. I said I'd keep an eye on it. Well, that wasn't quite enough. I've heard that two innocent whistleblowers have been eliminated to keep the operation secret. Christine was probably one of the two." He paused. "This all happened very quickly and was perpetrated by Manny Rufalo under the direction of Oscar Gleason. Now, a new interested party named Bob Hillman is pursuing his own investigation into the reason for the murders. He's asked me, as an aggrieved party, to help him pursue the matter. That's the 'sticky wicket' I wanted to talk over with you."

"I understand your quandary. I'm sure you've pieced it together and have a plan. Out with it."

"I think I'll just go along with Bob and try to keep him from undoing the carefully conceived drug program that's in place. I hope I can pull this off."

"Sounds like a plan, Eric. A bit vague, but until the threat begins to crystallize that's all you can do. Our objective here is to maintain a low profile and keep the operation going. Keep me posted. I am concerned that Gleason's outpost is becoming a dangerous wildcard. It's not essential to our enterprise, so it could be eliminated if it became too much of a liability."

"I understand, Alyssa. I understand."

CHAPTER EIGHTEEN

Pharmaceutical companies made the late spring meeting in Denver the event of the year for the industry. All major drug manufacturers and sellers were in attendance. Oscar Gleason and Larry Crandall used the occasion to have a private meeting in Larry's hotel room at which they would update each other on the past year's happenings in their respective companies. It was the only time they met each year and the only time they communicated at all.

"Nice to see you, Larry. I hope you had a good year. York enjoyed a solid year, meeting all its goals. We did have one unanticipated matter that required corrective action. I'll fill you in on the details after you've had a chance to bring me up to date on Sampson's past year."

"As usual, Oscar, I have very little to report. Sampson is doing quite well and I remain Mr. Outside, having little to do with the company's day-to-day operation. Mitch Trent is Mr. Inside and carries that responsibility. None of this, of course, is news to you. Your contract with Sampson is being fulfilled or else I would have heard otherwise. There is just one item of personal interest. My daughter passed away unexpectedly. It was quite a shock, as you might imagine. My wife and I took it especially hard and she's only now getting back on her feet. I mention this for no particular reason but thought you might want to at least be aware that my year wasn't without hardship."

"I'm very sorry to hear that, Larry. I know we keep a distance between us, but had I known I would have offered you and Elaine my condolences."

"Thanks, Oscar. Now what about that 'corrective action' you alluded to? It sounded ominous."

Oscar's mind was sending him warning signals. Something told him that he was near a precipice. Larry's daughter had died in circumstances unspecified and he was about to reveal that he had sanctioned a "corrective action" involving two young women. The equation wasn't complete but he didn't like the odds that Larry's daughter could somehow fit in here.

"Nothing of great importance, Larry. We took care of an information leak and that's that. Now why don't we go down to the reception area and blend into the crowd?"

Oscar hoped that Larry was put off the scent and would drop the subject. To his great relief, that was the case. They left the hotel room and parted company at the elevator with a handshake. Oscar was now intent on finding out the identities of the two women he had indeed ordered for elimination. His dread was that one would be named Crandall and he didn't know what would follow if Larry became aware of that.

CHAPTER NINETEEN

Bob's plan was to recreate the circumstances at Sampson that confronted Denise when she pursued her project. What was the product the men with the foot problem were working on? His theory somehow tied that product into the women's deaths. He and Eric discussed how they might get that information. For reasons he wouldn't specify, Bob didn't want to approach either Mitch or Larry. His only other contact at the company was Marjorie Cameron. She would have to be the source of the information or at least lead them to where it could be obtained. Eric indicated that Sampson would have a contract with each customer detailing what Sampson would deliver and what the terms of payment would be. Bob wondered if Marjorie would have access to those contracts.

Eric suggested they look at a copy of Sampson's annual report and hope the name of their audit firm would be on it. If so, Eric would approach Marjorie as a member of that firm wishing to review active contracts as they prepared for next year's audit. It might work.

The annual report was available on the Sampson website and the audit firm was included in the report. So far, so good. Now Eric would approach Marjorie and see if she had access to the contracts. At least their cover fiction made sense.

In anticipation of meeting Marjorie Cameron, Eric purchased a cellphone under the name Lowell Trebbins, his new identity. This was a precaution in case she needed to call him after he left her office with copies of the contracts.

The meeting came off without a hitch, although Marge was initially uneasy about giving out copies of the contracts. The documents were kept on file in a storeroom adjacent to Marjorie's and Mitch's offices. Marge's secretary made copies of the seven active contracts and Eric left with them comfortably fitted into a briefcase that bore his false initials, L.T.

Later that evening Eric and Bob met to go over the contracts.

"Okay, Eric, which one is likely to have been operative in the area of the low absenteeism that brought Denise to Sampson in the first place? As I recall it was a new contract that the two men with the foot problem had worked on for just several months."

"I think we can eliminate at least four of the seven, Bob. Those four were operative for over a year each. Of the remaining three, one was brand new and another was being processed in a remote annex of Sampson and only needed a small work crew. That really only leaves this one. A contract with York Chemical. It's just six months old. It's a good fit."

"Well, what's the product, Eric?"

"Some kind of additive for a wood sealer that York sells to large stores like Home Depot and Lowes. Doesn't sound very ominous to me.

What are we missing? How does this seemingly innocent wood sealer additive figure in two murders?"

"Let's try out a few angles, Eric, that would make this information work for us. Denise surely got this far and knew that two men working on the product had developed a similar problem in their feet. Chris had probably told her about the worker with nerve damage. They assumed the men had the same nerve problem. Something was toxic in the work environment. Most likely it was something inhaled."

"I agree, Bob. Knowing Denise, based on this suspicion she would have wanted OSHA to come in and check the work environment. Leibman's notes say as much. She would have notified someone in management, probably Mitch Trent, about the potential OSHA issue and expected the matter to be turned over to that agency. Marge Cameron was unaware of any OSHA contact. Hard to imagine HR not being aware of any such outside oversight. Maybe she wasn't in the loop."

"Why don't we just contact OSHA and ask them if they've visited Sampson or are planning to? I'll take that assignment, Eric."

"I think we're making progress, Bob. Let's meet again after you get the OSHA information."

CHAPTER TWENTY

Upon deep reflection, Elaine realized that her life with Larry was a senseless waste of her best years. Divorce made a lot of sense. Just being free of her loveless arrangement looked like a good option. It was, of course, conditional on a favorable divorce settlement so she could have a reasonable lifestyle while considering some form of employment. She had no definable skills although an attractive, middle-aged woman with above average intelligence and maturity could usually find some front office position meeting the public.

With Larry not due back from Denver until the next day, she was looking forward to an evening of theatre and dinner with Gabe, the divorced husband of a friend. He'd always shown an interest in her, even when married, and had responded to her invitation with enthusiasm. After the theater, Elaine planned to suggest they go to her pied-a-terre for a nightcap.

Elaine and Marge, being best friends, had an arrangement that Marge could use Elaine's pied-a-terre on nights that Elaine was not using it. This was supposed to be one of those nights. In any event, Elaine forgot to inform Marge of her intention to use the apartment this evening, a change in plan.

Marge and Mitch were in midtown and decided to make use of the available apartment. When they entered the apartment, unannounced, it was apparent that it was already in use. Mitch quietly made his way to the bedroom and cautiously looked in. He saw a very excited Elaine Crandall straddling a man who wasn't her husband. He retreated back to Marge and they exited the apartment.

Marge couldn't wait to hear what Mitch had seen. Once outside the building they stopped to talk.

"C'mon Mitch, out with it!"

"Okay, Marge. Our dear friend Elaine was screwing a guy with much gusto. I don't think the guy's name is Larry. That's all I can say."

CHAPTER TWENTY-ONE

Oscar scanned *The New York Times* metropolitan section from the days after the killings he had sanctioned. Eventually he found what he was looking for, a young woman, victim of a rape/murder in Central Park. He dreaded to read further but there it was; the victim's name was Denise Crandall. He closed his eyes and covered them with his hands.

"Jesus. What a fuck-up." He controlled his anger. Manny had no way of knowing the woman was Larry Crandall's daughter. He had never met Larry and, in view of Oscar's very limited contact with Larry, had no reason to associate the intended murder victim with the rather remote president of Sampson.

He couldn't lay this off on Manny, even if he wanted to. His only worry was what Larry would do if he ever found out. He straightened up in his chair and tried to think positive. Larry may never make the connection so it didn't pay to dwell on the negative. He tried to put it out of his mind and returned to the work on his desk.

CHAPTER TWENTY-TWO

OSHA had no record of any activity ongoing or past with Sampson Industries. It had taken several calls and transfers, but Bob was certain that OSHA had not been alerted to any problem at Sampson. So, either Denise didn't report her finding to Sampson management, or she did and the recipient chose not to move the matter along to OSHA. He found it hard to believe that Denise had not followed through when she learned about two workers with similar problems. Whom would she have told? And why did that individual bury the information?

Sitting in Eric's living room, the two men tried to construct a scenario that used all the information they had.

Bob laid out the pieces: (1) a toxic product was being manufactured at Sampson; (2) Denise and Chris became aware of that; (3) Denise likely reported that finding to someone at Sampson; (4) that someone chose not to bring in OSHA; (5) Denise, in reporting the problem, had revealed herself and Chris to be more knowledgeable than was safe; (6) the two women were eliminated.

"That's how I see it Eric."

"That's a fair summation, Bob. I see someone wanting to keep the toxic product flowing and secret. That person wouldn't want an OSHA investigation and wouldn't want Denise nosing around with dangerous information. The stakes had to be quite high though, to justify two murders. We need to know more about the product."

"I have an idea, Eric. I'll track the product to its destination and see if it's really only a benign additive in a wood finish product. None of this makes sense if that's all it is. There has to be more."

Eric could see the snowball rolling down the hill. As Bob put more of the pieces together, Eric could see his own position become less and less tenable. Alyssa had drawn a line in the sand. York was a disposable entity if it threatened the larger operation.

CHAPTER TWENTY-THREE

Mitch was sitting on dynamite information but didn't know how to make it work to his advantage. He knew that Oscar had pulled the plug on Larry's daughter. Larry hadn't a clue about that. He now also knew that Elaine was bedding down some guy. Another instance where Larry didn't have a clue.

What Mitch didn't know was that he grossly underestimated Larry Crandall. When Larry met with Oscar in Denver, the latter's hesitation to discuss his so called "corrective action" regarding an information leak had made him wonder why Oscar abruptly dropped the subject. He was obviously holding back something from Larry and that was uncharacteristic. Coming right after Larry had told him about his daughter's death, Larry pieced it together and suspected the action may have taken his daughter's life. This would have to be clarified.

When Larry asked Elaine why he was unable to reach her at home the night before he flew in from Denver, her explanation was specious. An innocent explanation would have sufficed but her answer was unnecessarily complex. As with Oscar's avoidance of an explanation to Larry, Elaine's rambling explanation only served to stimulate his imagination and lead him to wonder what she was hiding.

Larry had a keen sense of knowing when he was being misled or put off. In these two instances, his antennae had lit up. Mitch had no clue that Larry was about to uncover the information he, Mitch, was holding so close to his vest.

In a reverse situation, Mitch had no way of knowing that the illegitimate product he had uncovered at Sampson was not the only such product in the plant. Larry had garnered two other contracts for "mother" products, but had deliberately failed to bring Mitch along on the enterprise.

Yes, Mitch had underestimated his partner, as had many others. Larry's quiet, unassuming manner belied an intense desire to prove his superior intelligence, if only to himself.

CHAPTER TWENTY-FOUR

Armed only with the information in the contract he was investigating, Bob entered the loading dock at Sampson, hoping to locate the product he was curious about. He was dressed in jeans and a blue chambray shirt with a navy windbreaker.

"Hey, there. Can I help you?" A large man in coveralls with the Sampson logo over his vest pocket intercepted him before he could identify any of the shipments prepared for delivery.

"You probably can. I'm looking for the next shipment of this product."

Bob showed the man a contract copy. He studied it a minute and then pointed to a tightly wrapped parcel about six feet square, clearly labeled "York," sitting on a pallet.

"That's the one you're after. It's scheduled to leave here later to-day, so you're just in time. Now maybe you'll tell me who you are and why you're curious about this shipment."

"Sure. I'm Wes Crowder. I work for York and was sent here to see what shape the package was in before it was shipped. Our last ship-ment arrived damaged so we wanted to see if the next package left here in good shape. Any damage to this one on the receiving end would be the fault of the transporter and not the shipper. Looks okay to me. Mind if I wait to see it loaded on the truck?"

"Suit yourself. Shouldn't be more than an hour or so."

Bob retreated to his car in light rain and prepared to wait for the shipment to leave Sampson. He didn't have long to wait. The shipment was loaded into a van with "Sampson" inscribed on the side panels. The van received two other parcels of similar size and wrapping and then left the loading dock.

Bob followed at a discrete distance. Twenty minutes later the van arrived in downtown Yonkers and the parcel was unloaded at a receiving dock clearly marked "York Chemical." It didn't sit outside very long. It was loaded onto a motorized cart and driven inside.

So all that Bob had learned today was that the product in the contract had been delivered to the customer named in the contract.

Now what? he thought. "Guess I'll make a trip to Home Depot and see if they carry a wood finisher made by York Chemical."

He drove to the nearest Home Depot, went inside, and was greeted by a floor manager who steered him to the aisle with wood finish products. After a detailed inspection of a myriad of such products he identified one made by York Chemical. It appeared mainstream enough. The primary agent was polyurethane with added amounts of other chem-icals. The latter were not always specified and were not included in the advertising. He assumed the other chemicals in the York wood finish in-cluded the product Sampson sent to York. The basic chemical content was similar to several in the area. He decided to buy one and left with his prize catch.

When he and Eric met that evening, they were somewhat depressed by what Bob had learned or didn't learn. They were stymied.

Trying to find something to do that might brighten his outlook, Bob decided to give his reporter friend a call and take in a movie or something. He needed a break from his somewhat fruitless sleuthing. He gave her a call on her cellphone. She picked up the call and recognized the caller's name.

"Hey, Bob. Nice to hear from you. How goes it?"

"So-so, Leslie. I'm a better miner than detective. I was thinking of doing a movie and wondered if you were free and interested in something really make-believe, like a film at the Lincoln Center Cinema. Another choice would be the Joyce Dance Company down in Chelsea. Since this is last minute, tickets to the Philharmonic and New York City Ballet were sold out. Sorry I'm offering such a limited menu."

"Well, I'll forgive you this time. I probably should say I'm busy and not reveal my availability, but I'm game for a diversion and would love to see the Joyce Company. I'll meet you in front of the theatre on Ninth Avenue at 7:45 p.m. I assume the performance is at eight."

"You sound like a veteran New Yorker, Leslie, after only a year back in town. After the show we can grab a bite to eat in the Village. Okay?"

"More than okay. It sounds great, Bob. See you soon."

The Joyce was as exceptional as they expected. Now they were face to face in a small, below-street-level Italian restaurant in the West Village. They had nearly finished a bottle of Chianti before the veal saltimbocca arrived.

"This has been the diversion I needed, Leslie. I'm glad you were free. My effort at case solving has hit a wall. I'm no further ahead than I was when we first met and traded information. I've seen the contract for the work product Sampson was preparing and shipping to York. It's an additive to a wood finish that York markets under their name. Doesn't sound like something calling for a double murder, does it?"

"I thought we were on the verge of a breakthrough. Sometimes though the break comes unexpectedly from out of the blue. You just have to keep at it. I sound like an old philosopher but I've seen cases abruptly move forward when the outlook seemed hopeless."

"You're probably right, Leslie. And what are we doing bringing up the very matter we were trying to set aside for an evening diversion?"

"Right, Bob. Let's kill this bottle of wine and start on another."

Each was unsure how to move this casual engagement into more serious territory. Compatibility was more and more evident, making this a very promising beginning. For Leslie there was one weighty issue: would this develop into another long-distance romance? She'd managed the last one but it was a serious matter to consider. Bob was a West Coast guy and had strong western business interests. Her previous romantic interest was less distant and she had not been as committed to the D.C. area.

They finished the evening on a purely friendly basis with each harboring more serious thoughts about the other. Time would tell if they would be drawn into a more serious relationship.

CHAPTER TWENTY-FIVE

Late afternoon at Sampson found Marge and Mitch beginning to wind down. Most of the staff had gone home although Marge's secretary was still working. They sat in Mitch's office with the door closed.

"This guy, Bob Hillman, came into town and swept Denise off her feet. Marge, have you met him?"

"Yes, I have. He treated me to lunch and quizzed me about Denise's project at Sampson. I don't think he got his money's worth since I know very little about the study she was doing. You saw to that when you intercepted her reports and didn't let me read them. That's the story of my Bob Hillman meeting. A good poached salmon but not much else. Changing the subject, Mitch, I'm looking forward to lunch with Elaine tomorrow. She always gets on my case about my hooking up with married guys. Now I'd like to play that in reverse with married women hooking up with guys."

"Wait a minute. You're not supposed to know about her lover, married or single. Better keep that to yourself for the time being. I mean it."

"Of course, you're right. But it might be nice if we could double-date some time. I'm only kidding. Oh, by the way, how is the audit progressing?"

"What audit? We have several months before we start getting ready for that. What made you ask, Marge?"

"Some guy from our audit firm came by looking for contracts. He said they were beginning the process. My secretary gave him copies of our active contracts. It all seemed innocent enough. His name was Lowell Trebbins. I remember his name because I saw his initials on his briefcase."

"There is no audit underway, Marge. I would know. I'm going to call our audit firm right now and find out what's going on."

Mitch looked up his contacts on his cellphone. He dialed the number.

"This is Mitchell Trent at Sampson Industries. I'd like to be connected to the office of Arthur Golden."

After a pause, he continued. "Arthur, Mitch Trent here. I'll keep it brief. Do you have an employee named Lowell Trebbins?...You don't...Okay. One other question. Have you started our audit at this early date?...I didn't think so. Thanks for your time, Art.

"So someone walked out of here with copies of our active contracts. Describe the man for me, Marge."

"Six feet or so, light sandy colored hair, nice looking guy. No moustache or anything special to remember. Looked around forty or so. Had no wedding ring. I notice those things. That's about it."

"You might as well head home, Marge. I'll be staying here awhile pondering this curious event." Marge departed and Mitch was left to puzzle over that carefully planned scam.

He considered what anyone could learn from the contracts. The names of products and the names of customers attached to those products. The price of manufacture was included. That was about it. So how did that information merit a carefully staged robbery? He didn't have the answer but something told him that he had to get to the bottom of it.

He suddenly straightened up in his chair. Of course, the contracts included the chemical name of the product to be produced. One of them was a precursor chemical of an illegal drug they were making for York Chemical. One woman, maybe two, had been killed to protect the production of that chemical and safeguard its content. Now it appeared that someone was interested in unraveling the closely guarded cloak of secrecy surrounding it. Passing along this news would further ingratiate him with Manny. That would be his first call.

CHAPTER TWENTY-SIX

Sitting alone in his spacious Upper West Side apartment, Bob wondered how his life had spun in such different directions. Several months ago, he met a wonderful woman and they had even mentioned the "M word," something he had never contemplated with a woman friend. Now she was gone and he was seeing a new woman with a similar spunky personality. She made him feel uplifted and cheerful regardless of the mood he was in when they met. Before Leslie came into his life he was planning on returning to his home in San Francisco for good and beginning life anew. Now he was unsure. If he was a serious drinker he'd be stone drunk tonight, but that wasn't him. He was sober and trying to avoid thinking about his future.

Leslie was having similar thoughts about Bob. She'd been throwing herself into her work as a substitute for a deep relationship. Now she found herself entering one and seeing that work was a poor alternative.

After their initial exchange of information regarding Denise's murder they had avoided teaming up to work collaboratively on solving the mystery. Leslie didn't let their relationship slow down her pursuit of the story. She could function on two levels simultaneously, one as an increasingly close companion of Bob and the other as a relentless reporter pursuing a story with personal meaning to him.

CHAPTER TWENTY-SEVEN

Grayson's Gym on West 84th Street was a good distraction for Eric.

He spent an hour there each day, working out on a variety of weight machines. Today he was into the gym before 7:00 a.m. He wasn't the only early bird. He recognized most of the others. It was a muted group with each person doing his or her routine and showing little interest in small talk. For this early morning crowd the objective was to do the workout, get home to shower and dress, grab a quick breakfast, and move on to work.

As usual, the striking beauty in the workout crowd was pretending that her spandex one piece was not drawing any looks from the males in the gym. Eric marveled how the real lookers could look right through the oglers as if they weren't even worth a sideways glance or a quick glimpse in one of the many mirrors in the gym. She sported a ring on the second finger of her left hand that was an ambiguous piece of jewelry. She came alone and talked to no one. Eric knew her workout routine. She was into serious weight lifting. Her perfect figure belied her strength.

He decided to make a friendly effort at chipping away some of the ice encasing her. As he started over to her, a voice called out from behind him. "Lowell Trebbins. I remember you. Remember me? I'm the woman you scammed at Sampson to get copies of our contracts."

Eric stopped in his tracks and turned to where the voice was coming from. Marge was perspiring in her T-shirt and sweatpants. She fussed with her hair as she approached Eric and smiled in a friendly sort of way. He was relieved that this was not going to be an ugly confrontation. He recognized Marge even in this different venue and with quite different clothing. She was the same fortyish brunette with striking green eyes, but he was drawn toward her with less makeup and more natural clothes. Eric wasn't sure how to play this.

"I never expected to see you in this setting, Marge. New York's a big place but somehow coincidences still happen."

"Well, I belong to a gym in Yonkers near our plant but it has branches all over. Since I was planning on doing some shopping at Bloomingdales here in Manhattan, I thought I'd do my workout here at the 84th Street gym."

"I guess that's serendipity then. But before we get into the Lowell Trebbins story, why don't we meet for coffee at the Coffee Roaster down the block? It's a better atmosphere for friendly conversation. I think I can clear up the mystery. Believe me, it's not some sinister plot. "

"Good suggestion, Lowell. Give me twenty minutes." They left for their respective locker rooms.

Eric quickly called Bob. "You'll never guess who I'm having coffee with in twenty minutes. Marjorie Cameron from Sampson. She recognized me in the gym as the guy who got away with copies of the Sampson contracts. I don't think she knows who Eric Dinsmore is but I planned on continuing as Lowell Trebbins. I need a cover story for the contract scam. Do you have a good idea?...I didn't think so. I thought I'd invent a cover. Try this one: I work for a rival pharmaceutical/chemical company and was doing low level espionage. Spying on the competition to see who their customers are, what do you think?…Okay that's what I'm going with. If I can pull it off, she may prove to be a useful inside source. She may know more than she let on when you took her to lunch."

Bob issued a warning over the phone. "One last thing, Eric. When we had lunch she was quite protective of her boss, Mitch Trent. I couldn't pursue this angle but she is single and a good looking woman. I'd be careful here. She may be very close to him and information may flow easily from her to him. Let me know how it turns out."

Eric did the shower and clothes change in record time for him. Now he was seated opposite a much-refreshed Marjorie Cameron in Coffee Roaster. Wearing tights with a long, gray, cardigan sweater over a black T-shirt, Marjorie looked every bit the all-American woman you'd see in a *Land's End* catalogue. The only thing missing was a wedding ring.

"Well, Lowell, what are you going to con me out of this morning? Not much to lift at Coffee Roaster."

"I guess I deserve that, Marge. I was doing some low-level spying for a rival chemical company interested in learning about your customers. Let's put that contract scam behind us. Tell me a little about you. I'm a good listener."

"Okay, even some mean dudes in prison are given a second chance. I hope I won't regret this.

"I was born in San Diego and raised as an army brat, following my dad around the world until I was old enough to go it alone and start college. I majored in political science at Middlebury with a doctorate at Columbia and then found out the college world had little use for another poli-sci instructor. Sampson advertised for an HR person and was willing to give this novice a shot at the job. That's where I've been for the past ten years."

"I admire your honesty, Marge. My story is pretty simple. Born in Connecticut, bachelor's degree from Wesleyan, law degree from Fordham, and now in my fifteenth year in solo practice. The contract scam was a favor for a friend. It had nothing to do with my work."

After some light chitchat about favorite movies, vacations, and like, they knew a bit more about each other and saw similarities in their taste for pleasure.

"I'd like to sit here and talk some more, Lowell, but I'm meeting a friend. Glad we met. I saved you from being snubbed by Tatiana in the gym. She's a nice girl, but the ground around her feet is littered with the bodies of well-buffed guys. She'd only add you to the pile." They parted with a friendly handshake.

CHAPTER TWENTY-EIGHT

O scar listened intently as Manny relayed the information from Mitch. Oscar had two concerns. Number one was that someone was trying to determine what was so important at Sampson to get two women killed. Manny suspected it was the dead girl's boyfriend who didn't buy the random rape/murder explanation that the police initially had settled on. This was a threat but it had a long way to go before they needed to act.

The number two concern was the way Mitch Trent was becoming the uninvited keeper of too much information about their operation. He was not "family" and never would be. Manny saw him as a threat because his loyalty could not be guaranteed. Oscar and Manny were on the same wavelength about Mitch.

"Oscar, I need to know if you want to remove the threat that he represents. My own inclination is to move on this before he hurts us, not after."

"I understand your position, Manny. On the other hand, he is a valuable pair of eyes and ears very close to Sampson and our operation. So far he's been quick to call you as soon as anything suspicious happens. I think he likes the stipend we extend to him in exchange for his listening post. I'd ride with him a bit longer but have a quick response in case he seems to be straying or his threat becomes ominous. Can you accept that, Manny?"

"Your judgment is what we rely on. I'm always on board, Oscar. I guess we give him an extension before cutting him loose."

CHAPTER TWENTY-NINE

McDonough's Pub was a downscale watering hole a short distance up the road from the Sampson plant. It sat in a small cluster of stores that served the immediate needs of the local population. The big box stores and the internet were strangling the small retail merchants, but pubs like McDonough's still had the underpinnings to survive.

Bob had decided to try the pub as a possible gathering place for Sampson workers after the workday ended. The next nearest similar drinking hangout was several miles further away from the plant. This one had a friendly feel and Bob's intuition had proven him right.

He entered the pub dressed in jeans and a black flannel shirt and immediately felt as if he belonged. For all his wealth, Bob never left his mining camp manner far behind. He readily reverted from energy company mogul to hardhat mining hand.

The pub was crowded and noisy. He'd delayed his visit until he was sure the Sampson dayshift had let out. With some gentle pushing and twisting he made it to the bar and gave the harried bartender his order for two draft Stellas. Better get two now since getting to the bar for a second was going to be a challenge. While waiting, he tried some friendly banter with the guys on either side of him.

"Best part of the workday for me. I'm just doing deliveries in the area and saw all the cars parked outside. Figured it had to be a friendly spot. Name's Sid Parker. You part of the Sampson crowd?"

The drinker on his left was working on his third brew and feeling the faintly heady sensation that came with downing them in rapid succession. He gave Sid the closest attention he could muster.

"Right. Sampson's my second home. Wife's waiting at home for me so I better down this one and move along. All the guys here are Sampson and a friendly bunch we are." With that he downed the remainder of his drink, turned away and left.

Bob sized up the drinker on his right and introduced himself. "Sid Parker's my name. I'm looking for someone who works in the chemical processing area of Sampson." The man on his right was a ruddy, fiftyish guy with a friendly grin on his face. This happy hour with three-dollar beers had him in a relaxed frame of mind.

"Most of the guys here are in the chemical processing end of Sampson. I am and have been for over fifteen years." He wanted to talk shop so Bob let him have the floor, at least the very small piece of it they occupied.

"We work in teams on one project at a time so we form good friendships. All day at Sampson and after hours at McDonough's. What is it you want to know? We already have a union and the workers are mostly happy with their benefits."

"That's not what I'm after. I'm interested to learn if anything out of the ordinary took place at work over the past six months or so. I'm not a lawyer and not a reporter. You don't have to worry about talking to me. I'm not a company man either. I'm not even sure what I'm looking for but if you can recall anything unusual that happened in the last six months it might set me on a course. How about it?"

"Well, first time in my fifteen years they broke up a team of workers before a project was finished. Just traded us to other units like baseball players. Never explained why they made the change."

Bob sensed this could be important so he followed it up. "What happened to the project?"

"Nothing. Just continued with a different team and was restarted in the same worksite after the ventilation project was finished."

"Ventilation project? What was that about?"

"No big deal. Only took a week to update the exhaust system in that area. It was scheduled for later in the year but they moved it up and did it sooner. Made a difference I'm told."

"That's very interesting. So the project resumed with a new crew and the place returned to normal. Is that it?"

"I guess you could say that. Guy over there," and he pointed, "with the cane, was part of the team and didn't like being moved to a new site. He was given a less demanding job because of his legs and felt he was demoted even though his pay didn't change. Maybe you should talk to him. Name's Jim Healy. Nice guy."

"Thanks a lot. That was helpful. I didn't get your name."

"Ernie Blomquist. Nice to meet you, uh, uh, Sid."

"Ernie, have a few on me." He stuffed a ten-spot in Ernie's shirt pocket and moved on to the man with the cane.

Bob had a faint recollection of the Healy name. Of course, he was the coworker of Ethan Tyler who Mrs. Tyler indicated was seeing Doctor Christine Dinsmore.

"Hi, Jim. Got a minute? I was talking to Ernie over there and he suggested I talk with you about the changes at Sampson several months ago. Name's Sid Parker. I think Ernie saw no harm in talking to me.

I'm not a lawyer, reporter, or union spy, just a guy looking for information."

Healy was a tall, thin man with a furrowed brow. His hair was mostly brown but there wasn't much of it. He didn't have the happy face Bob saw on most of the pub drinkers."

"How'd the transfer work out for you, Jim?"

"Oh, is that what it's about? I shouldn't complain because they gave me light duty. Told me they were worried I might fall and hurt myself. They seemed to know about my condition, the foot thing. Don't know how they knew, but they did. So I was moved out and given an easy job."

"So how have the feet been since the transfer? I see the cane."

"Well, I must say they're no worse. Not much better either."

"Jim, who was making these decisions?"

"Probably Mitch Trent. He's the guy oversees all the internal operations. I'd bet it was his decision."

"That's helpful, Jim. Thanks for talking to me."

Again, he stuffed a ten-spot in a shirt pocket and moved to the exit. Back in his car he reflected on what he'd learned. Someone had ordered a staffing change in the area where Jim Healy and presumably Ethan Tyler worked. A rush had been put on the ventilation upgrade in the area.

The someone who ordered these changes had likely been put on notice by Denise that there was a problem with some toxic agent in the area. Rather than notify OSHA, he or she decided to make corrective changes in the area and resume work on the contract as quickly as possible. The someone most likely was COO Mitch Trent, the guy who said Denise had not uncovered any important information. He was obviously intent on hiding something about the operation in that area and that need for secrecy may have cost Denise her life. Since Christine had been in possession of the same critical information, it was safe to assume that her life had been taken for the same reason.

CHAPTER THIRTY

Sleep wasn't coming easy to Leslie. She was convinced the two women weren't killed to keep up production of a wood sealer component. The Sampson product had to be more than that. A lot more. She kept grinding at it.

Her working theory was that Sampson shipped a product to York Chemical. York then took off some component of the product and used the remainder in the wood sealer they sold commercially. If this theory was correct, she'd need a sample of the product Sampson shipped and a sample of the final product York sold. She would analyze each and the difference in composition between the Sampson additive in the wood sealer and the product Sampson sent to York would tell the story. She could use the can of sealer Bob had bought at Home Depot to, hopefully, identify the final product. What she needed was a sample of what

Sampson sent to York. She wasn't sure how she'd obtain that but she was thinking.

Looking ahead, she realized that the removed component would have to be the closely guarded secret that the two women had been murdered to protect. What could be that valuable and had to be kept secret? An illegal drug was the only item she could imagine having such value. If that was the answer, she knew from experience that they were meddling in a game that was run by very dangerous men who didn't take kindly to anyone who threatened their very lucrative livelihood. She'd have to lay it on heavy to Bob and Eric that the opposing players in this game took no prisoners.

The next morning, her plan was taking form. Sitting in a car borrowed from a fellow *Times* employee, Leah Rosen, Leslie sat a safe distance from Sampson observing the loading dock through binoculars. Her interest wasn't in the dock itself but in the Sampson van that was used to pick up parcels and make deliveries. She would try to hitch a ride when it was carrying a parcel destined for York Chemical.

After two long hours, a van labeled "Sampson" drove up to the dock.

She drove around to the front of the Sampson building, out of sight of the loading area. She parked in the visitors' parking area and hustled around the building toward the loading dock. Before turning the last corner, she slowed down and approached the dock at a leisurely pace. The driver of the van was helping load a parcel labeled "York" into the back of the van. Leslie approached casually and addressed the driver as he was closing the van's rear doors.

"Hello. I was wondering if I could hitch a ride with you to York. I have some business there and my car won't be back here for a few hours."

The driver looked her over briefly. He saw a well-groomed, good-looking woman in a dark gray suit and pale blue blouse.

"Don't see why not. I wouldn't mind some company on the run to York. Just hop in. I have to sign for the parcel and then we'll be on the way. Name's Jerry, short for Jeremiah."

"Great, Jerry. This'll save me a lot of time. Call me Nan."

Leslie got into the passenger seat in the van, then turned and took a quick look at the parcel heading for York. She could easily reach it from her seat just by turning. Jerry climbed into the driver's seat and they took off.

"Hey, Jerry, how about a quick stop to pick up some beers? I'd like to treat you to one to thank you for this favor."

"Can't spare the time, Nan, but I can stop and pick up a six-pack for us to work on while we drive. I know where I can park and get the beer. Done it before and will do it again. That okay with you?"

"Sounds better than okay. I'll even let you pick the brew as long as you let me pay. This twenty should do the trick."

Leslie tucked a twenty-dollar bill in Jerry's waistband. After a short drive, Jerry pulled into a strip mall and parked head-on in front of Rebello's Package Store.

"Won't be but a minute, Nan."

Jerry left the van and ran into the package store. Leslie quickly reached into her briefcase and took out a small leather case containing a syringe and needle. She affixed the needle to the syringe, turned in her seat and stuck the needle into one of the containers in the parcel they were delivering to York. She quickly filled the syringe, pulled the needle out of the container, capped the syringe, and put it back in the case she carried it in. She then applied a tiny amount of gum-like substance to seal the hole and prevent any leakage. The whole operation took less than a minute and was finished before Jerry emerged from the store carrying the six-pack. They then drove on to York and each finished a bottle of Heineken by the time they arrived. Jerry and Nan parted company with a friendly handshake.

"Any time you need a ride give me a call, Nan, at this number." Jerry handed Leslie a card with Sampson's name and transport's phone number.

Leslie entered the building that housed York but didn't go any further. She sat down in the lobby and waited for Jerry to drive off. She then called Uber and arranged to be taken back to Sampson in thirty minutes.

The sample was hand-delivered to an analytic lab along with a sample of the wood sealer Bob had purchased.

CHAPTER THIRTY-ONE

The television set was playing in the background as Marjorie Cameron read through her pile of unread *New Yorker* magazines. She'd ordered in a bunch of appetizers from the local Japanese restaurant. Now she stopped reading and gave her third glass of wine some serious attention. Brooding had become a more frequent activity on these lonely nights. What she brooded about was the lack of direction and a future in her life.

She'd been very scholarly in college and graduate school, but had ended up working for a minor league chemical company. Her boss had shoved her aside when an interesting problem appeared in her domain. Sleeping with him only made it worse. She followed his instruction and stayed away from the problem because she wanted to please him. Elaine was right. Giving herself to a married man who voiced no interest in leaving his wife was the deadest dead-end. Now was the time to get real.

She was closing in on forty and didn't have anything to show for it. She didn't love Mitch and he certainly didn't love her. So now what? This guy, Lowell Trebbins, was an interesting find. She could see more of him and maybe start a fresh path for herself. There were no restraints on her. Sex was one hook that worked for her, but there was more to her than that. It seemed a light had suddenly gone on and illuminated her life. She had no one to blame but herself for the rut she was in. Now she would have to lift herself out of the rut.

"Think positive, Marge. You've got a lot going for you. Just don't settle for a life that's less than you can create for yourself," was the advice she arrived at for herself.

She picked up the phone and dialed the number Lowell had given to her when he scammed the office. The phone asked for a message after four rings. "Hello, Lowell. This is Marge from the Coffee Roaster. I was wondering if we could continue our conversation over another cup of coffee. If you're interested, name the place and pick a time. I'm pretty available."

Eric Dinsmore, a.k.a. Lowell Trebbins, picked up the message and turned it over in his mind. This woman, Marge Cameron, was potentially useful as an inside contact at Sampson, but he wasn't thinking business. He was conflicted. Chris was gone less than a year and presumed dead. He didn't feel quite ready to start meeting women and beginning a new social life. Nevertheless, he pictured Marge's face and her magnetic green eyes. He returned the call and set up a date for some more conversation.

CHAPTER THIRTY-TWO

The stop sign at the corner of Topfield and Haddam was barely visible through the drooping branches of the maple trees after the rain. Jerry Ozinski was distracted by the bottle of beer he was trying to finish so he missed the full stop. He also had the bad luck to do it just as Officer Cunningham wiped the mustard from his mouth in the police car sitting at the corner. The short siren caught Jerry's attention. He pulled the van over and hid the bottle under his seat.

Cunningham wrote him a ticket for running a stop sign. He cautioned Jerry about driving under the influence since the smell of beer in the van was quite strong. On second thought, he asked Jerry to step out of the van so he could search it for the source of the smell. It didn't take long for him to find the leaking beer bottle under the driver's seat and the six-pack with three empties in the cargo space of the van. A few simple tests told the officer that Jerry was not impaired but that he was showing signs of heading there.

He decided to give him a doomsday warning about drinking and driving but not write it up. He would have a few words with his employer, off the record. He didn't want to threaten the guy's job, but he didn't want a driver with a commercial license driving and drinking. Jerry was relieved.

Mitch Trent knew Jerry's family so he didn't give him a serious dressing down the next day. He did make it clear that the drinking on the job had to end. Jerry was sufficiently chastised in the COO's eyes, so he thought their brief one-on-one was over when he offered a lame excuse.

"I've been pretty good about drinking in the van, Mr. Trent, until some visitor to Sampson asked me for a ride to York. I was in an obliging mood so we drove together. She was kind enough to buy me a six-pack on our way over, so we shared a few in the van. That sort of got me started."

Mitch was on guard.

"Tell me about the woman who asked for a ride. Where was she coming from? You said she was a visitor to Sampson. How did you know that?"

"Well, she was coming from the front of the building, so I assumed she had come out from there. She was dressed in a suit and looked like a person who might have had business inside. She said she had business at York and asked if I could drive her over. She said her ride wouldn't be back for a few hours so I could save her some time. When we got there, she went inside and that was the last I saw her."

"How did she know you were heading to York?"

"That's a good question. She must have seen the parcel on the loading dock that was clearly labeled 'York.' Or maybe someone inside told her our van makes frequent trips over to York. I don't know how she knew. I'm only guessing."

"Last thing, Jerry. Describe this woman for me."

"A good-looker, about thirty-five. About five foot six with a nice body. Oh, yeah. She said her name was Nan. No last name."

Mitch was not sure what to make of this. He'd try to check this woman out but had little to go on. Security cameras might help but he wasn't sure how this ride with Jerry could be made into anything of concern. It all came back to what someone could gain from a ride with Jerry. The fact that the ride was between two sites linked in a drug scheme didn't let him write it off as a random bit of nonsense.

"Wait a minute, Jerry. Was she ever alone in the van without you? You said she bought you a six-pack. Who actually bought the six-pack?"

"Well, I did, but she paid for it. That's what I meant when I said she bought me a six-pack."

"So she was alone in the van when you went into a store to get the beer. Am I right, Jerry?"

"Yeah, but what harm was there in that? It only took a couple of minutes."

"No problem, Jerry. You can go now. Just remember, no beer in the van when you're on the job."

Jerry left. Mitch was left to wonder what that stranger could have gained from the ride and a few minutes alone in the van with the cargo destined for York. Much as he wanted to see it as an innocent happening, it bore too many signs of something well-planned and potentially threatening. Before calling Manny he wanted to go over the security tapes and see what he could figure out for himself.

The tapes were easily retrieved and reviewed in the Sampson security office. Since he knew the date and time of interest it was easy to locate the section of tape he wanted. There wasn't a lot of foot traffic into the Sampson front lobby so he readily identified a woman who was very likely Jerry's rider. He printed out the best picture of her from the tape, but, not surprisingly, it was a poor face shot when it was blown up to a usable size.

He stopped for a minute then looked at the tape a few more times. The camera had a good view of the parking area where Sampson management folk parked. The chemical workers parked in another lot more convenient to their locker room and work area. There were only eight cars in the parking lot and he could roughly make out their license numbers. He painstakingly wrote down each number, leaving blank those numbers he couldn't decipher. His batting average was pretty good. Seven of the eight were fairly complete and the one missing plate was mostly obscured by plants. He could only make out one or two numbers on that plate.

Armed with his list of license plate numbers he made his rounds of the management area, asking workers if any of the numbers identified their car. He could account for all but one of the cars. Several workers carpooled, so he also accounted for just about all the management staff. The one car not claimed by anyone was very likely the car Jerry's rider said she had to wait several hours for. That lie validated his suspicion that something not so innocent had taken place.

His friend at the Department of Motor Vehicles would be happy to track down the owner of the vehicle. He owed Mitch a favor and now he could deliver. Once he had a name, he'd give Manny a call.

CHAPTER THIRTY-THREE

The quick response to her voicemail gave Marge reason to think Lowell, a.k.a. Eric, was interested in pursuing some kind of relationship. Just what kind was unclear, but that was what dating was all about.

She picked out an outfit that matched up with an informal Upper West Side, Middle Eastern restaurant.

Marge couldn't have done any better in shaping the evening from her point of view. She could sense his relaxed state and attributed this to a bona-fide attraction to her. She had an inkling of this at the Coffee Roaster.

Their conversation was lighthearted and reflected a shared sense of humor. Marge was not going to play hard to get. If he was really interested, and she could sense he was, she'd help him move them along.

"Lowell, you live near here, don't you?" Marge offered this not-so-subtle hint for being invited up to his apartment. Not surprisingly, it was the slight shove Lowell needed to get off the dime and think he was making the move.

"Yeah, I live a few blocks south of here. Why don't we go to my place and have a nightcap or two?"

"Good idea, Lowell." They got their coats and decided to walk to his building since it was only five short blocks away.

Eric had purged his apartment of Chris memorabilia. Having her pictures and clothes around had been too painful for him in the early weeks after her disappearance. He had done another apartment sweep in anticipation of his date with Marge. Her comment about where he lived gave him the opening he needed to invite her up. She probably thought he didn't see through it. He liked the way she could be subtle and forward at the same time. And those green eyes.

They settled into the sofa in the living room with drinks in hand. Eric had decided to come clean. "Marge, I have to level with you about who I am. I don't want to start a friendship under false pretenses. Please bear with me." She looked at him very intensely, afraid that their very early relationship was about to come to a crashing end.

"My name is Eric Dinsmore. I'm an attorney. I was happily married for six years and then my wife mysteriously disappeared a number of months ago. The police believe she was probably murdered but no trace of her has ever been found. Now for the really tough part. She was a very close friend of Denise Crandall who was murdered the same day my wife, Chris, disappeared."

He paused and Marge leaned forward as an expression of increased interest. He could tell he had her full attention.

"You're beginning to see where this is going. Her close friend Bob Hillman and I have been trying to solve the mystery of these two deaths. My scam in your office to get those contracts was part of our search. We believe that the two women were killed because they had innocently uncovered information that threatened to expose some illegal activity at Sampson. That's my true story. You met me at the gym and that offered us an opportunity to cultivate you as a potential inside source of information at Sampson. You and I have gone beyond that pretense. I want us to be on firm footing if you let tonight go forward."

"Wow. I thought you were ending us right here. First, I'm very sad about your wife and your marriage. I assume there were no children. The Sampson story, though, is a bit beyond me. For the moment, I'd like to have our personal lives move on and keep Sampson apart from us. Maybe I'll become a part of your search team, but not tonight. I need some time to digest all this. I just want to keep us moving in the direction we've been heading.

"I'm glad I got that off my chest, Marge. There is only one thing I have to ask. Keep this secret. I mean really secret. No one, especially at Sampson, can know about what Bob and I are doing."

"Secret it is. And I mean *really* secret."

CHAPTER THIRTY-FOUR

It was late afternoon and Sampson management people were emptying out the office wing of the building. Mitch was making no move to join the migration home. He was wondering why Marge had been so cool toward him of late. She'd cancelled their regular tryst and gave him a lame excuse. Her office was only a few steps from his, but he'd be damned if he was going to make an effort to find out what was troubling her. He missed their mid-afternoon romps so it took some effort to restrain himself.

His telephone rang and he saw it was the DMV calling him. He picked up the phone and pushed Marge out of his thoughts.

"Connor, you old devil. That didn't take long. Tell me what you got."

"Nothing earth-shaking, Mitch. The plate you gave me belongs to Leah Rosen who lives at 584 West 104th Street in Manhattan. That's about it."

"Connor, that's all I needed. You're a pal indeed. I owe you. Many thanks."

Now, armed with a name he put in a call to Manny.

"Manny Rufalo here."

"Manny, this is Mitch. I want to run something by you that may be important." He proceeded to relate the story of the woman who bummed a ride with Jerry. As he told it he began to see the importance of the setup and the brief moment when Jerry left the van to buy a six-pack. Mitch then went on to gloat about how he obtained the hitchhiker's identity.

"That's very interesting, Mitch. You did a good job. Better than good, you did a great job. The address is helpful. You were wise to not let the innocent remark by your driver slip past you."

Manny knew how much Mitch liked to be stroked so he laid it on.

Aside from that, he was more than a little curious about Leah Rosen and how she figured in this never-ending Sampson tale. He would initiate some appropriate action.

CHAPTER THIRTY-FIVE

The email Leslie had been waiting for finally hit her computer. She surprised even herself at how eager she was to find out what the chemical analysis had shown. The report from Crane Analytic was three pages long and full of technical data well beyond her knowledge and interest. The bottom line was succinctly stated in the summary statement that was intended for a layman like herself. The product York received was principally compound A. The final product out of York, the wood finish, was largely polyurethane, but also contained a modified compound A, now largely stripped of a component. She called the missing component compound B.

This was the smoking gun she had suspected. The next step would be to determine the properties of the missing component. For this she would enlist the help of a pharmacologist at Columbia University.

She forwarded the report to Bob Hillman along with her stated intention to further pursue investigation of the missing chemical component. She also explained how she'd obtained the sample.

The pieces were falling into place. She had little doubt that the chemical would possess properties making it a valuable item on the street. Sometimes being an investigative reporter had its moments of satisfaction.

CHAPTER THIRTY-SIX

A reporter's nose for news can sometimes pick up a scent well worth following. In this case her nose was telling her that the problem at Sampson was the manufacture of a cleverly concealed illegal drug. Denise Crandall and her physician friend had innocently jeopardized that process. They were innocent in the sense that their concern about worker health or safety was going to focus attention where it wasn't wanted. They weren't aware of the illegal drug being manufactured but that didn't matter to those concerned with imposing the utmost secrecy on the process.

The trouble with this reading of the situation was her utter lack of proof. Until she had some tangible evidence there was no story to write.

Business needs out on the West Coast diverted Bob's attention from the Sampson matter for several days. By the time he got to his emails, the message from Leslie was already two days old. He cursed himself for letting his attention be diverted from their case. Her email was dynamite. He called her.

"Leslie, that's great information. Why didn't you tell me what you were going to do?"

"I thought you'd try to talk me out of it. It did sound a bit crazy but it was the step we needed to take. Now we know what we're up against. Don't hold it against me that I did it without your knowledge."

"Quite the opposite, Leslie. I admire your guts and determination to follow your instincts. My concern is for your safety. Remember, the secret was worth killing for. I don't like to see you get in the cross-hairs of the drug crowd."

"Believe me, Bob, I'm not after any attention from the people running this drug operation. I'm all low-profile on this one. You're the only person I've told about my adventure and the results of the chemical analysis."

"How can you be sure no one saw you or traced your car at Sampson? The fellow you hitched the ride with may have passed the information on to some worker at Sampson."

"He doesn't know my name and seemed satisfied with the line I fed him. I can't see him as any threat to me."

"Please, no more solo adventures without discussing them with me beforehand. I care about you."

"I sensed that and share the feeling, Bob. I hope you'll be back soon so we can plan the next move. I miss you."

CHAPTER THIRTY-SEVEN

Leah Rosen picked up her mail and climbed three flights of stairs to her studio apartment. As soon as she entered a hand was placed over her mouth to prevent her from screaming. She dropped her mail and handbag and was close to fainting from fright. The three men in her apartment were total strangers to her.

She was placed in a chair and her hands tied in front of her.

"Can we talk, Ms. Rosen, without having to worry about you screaming? This can go easy on you if you cooperate." The dark-haired man with a sallow complexion spoke very calmly. He was trying his best to allow her to gain some composure. "I have several questions to ask you and I want simple answers. Are you prepared to cooperate so we can take the hand off your mouth? Just nod yes and we can proceed."

Leah nodded and the hand over her mouth was removed. She was too afraid to speak.

"Leah, why were you at Sampson Industries last week?"

"I have no idea what you're talking about. You'll have to explain to me what's going on. I don't know what Sampson Industries is. Are you sure I'm the person you want to talk to?"

Manny hesitated. He was unsure about this person's role in the hitchhiker incident. Could they have the wrong person?

"Let's start again, Leah. Your car was seen at Sampson Industries last week. Why were you there?"

"So that's it. I haven't used my car in over two weeks. And I have no idea where this Sampson Industries is located. See, you *do* have the wrong person."

Manny was growing impatient.

"Okay, one more try. Why did you hitch a ride in the van to York?"

Leah hesitated. She was very frightened. These guys were not going to be kind to her if she was evasive. She couldn't think of a good answer.

"I do lend my car to friends so one of them may have used it last week."

Manny was trying to be patient. He was following Oscar's advice and wanted to avoid making waves unless necessary.

"Okay. Give me a few names, Leah. This may work out okay for you. Now you're being helpful. The names?"

Leah could only think of Leslie Nugent and Arnie Williams. She passed these names on to Manny.

"Leah, I assume that Arnie is a man so that leaves Leslie Nugent. I want you to give her a call now and ask if she borrowed your car last week. Tell her you're lending it to a friend for two weeks so it won't be available until the last week of this month. Call her Leah."

Leah saw no way out of this. She was too frightened not to comply. The call to Leslie's cell was answered promptly and she confirmed that she had borrowed the car last week. Manny didn't want to push it

any further and put the Nugent woman on alert. He felt certain this accounted for the car being at Sampson and identified the hitchhiker.

"We have to go now, Leah. You've been very helpful."

Leah was much relieved. Her hands were untied.

Manny gave a nod to one of the men who abruptly held a pillow
over Leah's face and put a bullet into the back of her head. The men left.
There was no witness to this interrogation and the Nugent woman would
not be warned by Leah Rosen.

Leslie was unable to reach Leah for two days. She didn't answer
her phone. Texts and emails went unanswered. Her workplace was concerned about her as well and had no clue why she was not showing up.

Leah was a loner and had no close family. Leslie was one of her
few friends and she had only known Leah for several months.

Leslie went to Leah's apartment and let herself in with the key
Leah had given her. The car keys came with a copy of the apartment key.

Leslie found the body on the living room floor lying face down
in a large pool of blood. She was stunned for a moment but could see
from the congealed blood pool that this wasn't a fresh kill. That eased her
concern that the killer could still be in the apartment. She stared at
Leah's body and began to sob.

It was murder, pure and simple. But why? Poor Leah. She had no
enemies that Leslie knew of. She worked in advertising at the paper and
was as non-confrontational as a person could be. So why would anyone
murder Leah Rosen?

She put the keys on the kitchen table. That triggered a thought in
her mind. *I used her car to go out to Sampson. She probably didn't know I was
going to borrow it. That was our arrangement. She had given me a set of car keys
to keep and her permission to take the car for a few hours whenever I needed it.
That was no oftener than once every other month. I would just bring it back that
same day to its garage parking space.*

Leslie was imagining how her use of the car could have been in any way responsible for her death. *I left it for a few hours at Sampson and no one took any notice.* Or did they? Surveillance cameras were likely all around the building. She hadn't taken notice of them.

If the car was the connection to the murder then she, not Leah, was probably the person the killer or killers had been after. Sure, someone else may have borrowed the car in the interim and who knows how that could connect to the murder. Still, connecting Sampson to the killing began to make sense in the context of what she was investigating.

She called the police and sat in the apartment until they arrived. When they did, she didn't share any information about the Sampson matter. It was all speculative so she kept it to herself.

Leslie left the murder scene with a very uneasy feeling. She had no doubt that Leah's call to her had been made under duress and that the killer now had her identity. They undoubtedly guessed that she'd hitched a ride from Sampson to York and would want to know what she'd gotten out of that. It wasn't hard to imagine that they might suspect she was after a sample of the product the van was taking to York. Bob had warned her not to get in the crosshairs of the drug crowd and now that's exactly where she was.

She called Bob and explained the situation to him. They agreed she should keep away from her apartment. She cabbed over to his building and tried to relax in his arms. Her tension was palpable. He realized no amount of assurance was going to set her mind completely at ease. He'd do his best, though, and try to provide her with safe passage to and from work.

The possibility that she could be followed from work back to Bob's apartment had to be considered. Bob hired a private investigator whose sole job would be to transport Leslie to work and from work back to some apartment. His focus would be principally to avoid being followed from work. They discussed various ploys and evasive maneuvers. Bob and Leslie were satisfied that the P.I. knew what to do. They realized that he couldn't use his car since it could be traced and the P.I. would then become vulnerable to threats and possible interception. They would use cabs and Ubers.

They agreed that it would be wise for her to stay at an apartment separate from Bob on the chance that the two of them could be connected by past association. They rented a studio apartment nearby in a secure building.

Leslie then confessed to Bob that she carried a small caliber handgun in her purse. She had a license for it based on the type of stories and venues she often ventured into. Chan had helped her obtain the license and select a weapon. He had also taken her on a few target practice sessions, assuring himself that the weapon was in good hands.

CHAPTER THIRTY-EIGHT

"Getting us handguns will set my mind a bit at ease, Eric. The guys we're mixing with are not amateurs like us. I'll still feel better if we're armed and familiar with our weapons. The sooner we get the hardware, the better. I'll leave that to you, Eric. You must have some connections who can help us out."

"I'll take care of it, Bob. I know someone who I can use. Now, let's discuss the email Leslie sent to you."

"I think it's pretty clear what's been going on, Eric. Leslie got the crucial sample and the report shows that York was extracting a component from the mother chemical sent to them from Sampson. Is it the jewel we thought it was? An illegal drug whose manufacture had to be protected from discovery? Leslie is apparently pursuing that with a pharmacologist at Columbia."

"Whenever I think about it, Bob, my heart goes out to the two women who innocently threatened the enterprise they stumbled on. My next reaction is rage."

"Eric, I'm with you all the way on this. My rage is also rising to the top. Let's not let it destroy the case we're building. We need to wait until Leslie gets the low-down on the chemical."

Bob held his head in his hands and stared at the floor. Something was missing here.

"Eric, solving the chemical puzzle isn't going to be enough. I want to know who bears the responsibility for the killings. And then I want there to be payback."

"Bob, I feel exactly the same."

Eric could feel his role in this chase coming to an end. He was too conflicted to remain Bob's partner. His allegiance was to Alyssa and the company. His job had been to monitor the progress Bob was making and then head it off before he blew the cover off the York operation. That was a threat to the larger organization and Bob, along with Leslie Nugent, were getting too close for comfort. He would discuss this with Alyssa.

CHAPTER THIRTY-NINE

Having the hitchhiker's identity was one thing, knowing what to do with the information was something else. Manny recognized his instinct to take a violent approach to anything at all threatening. For some reason he held back and decided to ask Oscar for advice. He surprised even himself at the uncharacteristic restraint he was showing.

The sun was setting across the Hudson over New Jersey. Oscar had arranged to meet Manny at a small park along the river. Now they sat on a bench watching the glorious sunset.

"Quite magnificent, don't you think, Manny?"

"I agree, Oscar, but that's not why I wanted to see you. I need your advice about a matter that only came up yesterday. You know that hitchhiker I mentioned to you, the one that hitched a ride with the courier from Sampson to York? We were unsure what to make of it but thought it was not an insignificant event. Well, I now know the hitchhiker's identity and don't know how to deal with her. That's why I wanted to see you."

Oscar watched the sun set behind the Palisades. The pause in the conversation taxed Manny's patience but he knew better than to assume his boss was daydreaming. Oscar often took his time and painstakingly thought through his response before speaking. Manny had learned to curb his impatience.

"I think you need to ask this person what she was doing in the van. What did she learn, if anything, that could pose a threat to us? This is not a time for deadly force. We need information. The question is how to get that information. It was a good thing you didn't lash out and eliminate the woman. She may have passed on the information she went after. A corpse is difficult to interrogate."

"So you're suggesting I snatch her and get that information out of her before finishing her off?"

"Not exactly. More killings only leave a better-defined trail for the police. First get the information, then, depending on what you learn we can decide if any further action would be called for."

"She may not be easy to snatch in Manhattan. Especially if she's on alert."

"Manny, why should she be on alert? What haven't you told me?"

"Okay. Mitch did some good detective work. He traced the car she used back to its owner. I thought the woman who owned the car was the hitchhiker at first. When it became apparent she had lent the car to the real hitchhiker, I got her to give us that person's name. We offed her at this point so she couldn't warn the hitchhiker about the danger she had been put in. The owner also wouldn't be able to identify me. Maybe I was too quick to act here. I don't know."

"I don't know either, Manny, but I suspect the woman who borrowed the car may figure out that her friend was killed instead of her and is now very much on alert. In that case, I agree that snatching her may prove difficult. But that's water under the bridge. Find her and solve the snatching dilemma."

"I'll do my best, Oscar."

CHAPTER FORTY

Mitch didn't know what to make of Marge's sudden disinterest in him. They'd been going along smoothly and then she began to turn down his offers of playtime in the afternoon. She was cordial but there was no longer any sense of the intimacy that had been a part of their relationship. He couldn't figure it out and his ego didn't let him ask her directly. In simple terms, she had cooled on him.

He tried to rewarm his relationship with his wife, Brenda, but after being ignored for so long she had built a life for herself that didn't include him. He felt lonely and didn't know how to restart his life. He decided to follow Marge to see if there was a new guy in her life. That could explain her cold shoulder, even though he'd be hurt if that was the case.

Marge was preparing to leave the office at the end of the day. Mitch was going to follow her and see where she led him.

The drive into Manhattan was slow, but he easily followed her to her apartment house. Double-parked across the street, he waited for her to emerge, knowing that she might be staying in this evening. He didn't have anywhere to go, so time was of little consequence.

He didn't have long to wait. She came out in a different dress and hailed a cab. Obviously she was heading out to meet someone. He followed the cab down to Greenwich Village where she got out and was greeted with a warm hug and kiss by some guy he never saw before. They went into the Peruvian restaurant on the corner.

It would take several hours before they finished dinner but he'd wait and follow Marge's guy home. He didn't have anything else going on that needed his attention.

"So this is what P.I.s do," he mused. "Wait and then wait some more."

Eventually the couple emerged and hopped in a cab. Mitch followed them through the tangled streets of the West Village onto the West Side Drive and up into the Upper West Side. Somewhere in the high nineties they were dropped off and went into a doorman-guarded, modern high-rise apartment building. He'd been to Marge's place so he safely assumed this was the guy's building. Double-parked, he quickly ran to the building's front door. He could see the couple board an elevator and go up to the tenth floor. That was the best he could do without encountering the doorman.

He quickly checked the list of apartments on the call-up directory. There were six apartments on the tenth floor. He excluded the two with Asian names. The remaining four names meant nothing to him, except one did seem familiar. "Dinsmore" was triggering a response in his memory but he couldn't make any connection. The more he tried to place it, the more certain he became that it was important. He'd let it go for now, but he was determined to recall its significance as soon as possible.

CHAPTER FORTY-ONE

Once again Mitch delivered important information to York Chemical.

Manny met with Mitch and told him they were tracking down the spy. He didn't tell Mitch that they learned very little in the process. Out of idle curiosity, Mitch floated the name "Dinsmore" to Manny. He was surprised when Manny had a response similar to his own.

"That name is familiar, but I can't place it. Where did you come across it?"

Mitch was not in the habit of giving Manny information without having a sense where it could lead. He worried about potential consequences for him.

"Wish I could tell you, Manny. It's just one of those things that pops out and drives you insane trying to find a context to fit it into."

"Wait a minute, Mitch. That's the name of the lady doctor you mentioned when you told us about the other woman and her interest in the Sampson work area where our product was being made. Okay, Mitch. Out with it. This sounds like trouble. Where did you come across the name of that woman?"

Mitch was cornered and could see no way out without telling Manny about his jealous trailing of Marge to find out if she was seeing a new guy in place of him.

"Wait a minute, Mitch. This is getting out of hand. You're telling me the guy on this date is the husband of the Dinsmore doctor. I can stretch coincidence as far as anyone but this busts even my imagination. And what are you doing in this mix? Trailing a girlfriend who is now hanging on the arm of the Dinsmore widower? And what are you not telling me? The woman who dumped you…how is she connected?"

"She works at Sampson. She's the HR person."

"Great. Mitch, you're a never ending source of mind bending information. How much does this little lady know about our Sampson operation?"

"Nothing, as far as I know. I have no idea about the guy though. I assume he has an interest in knowing more about the deaths and what, if any, connection there is to Sampson. I agree with you that there are too many connections here to ignore."

"Okay, Mitch. Here's what you're going to do with all this info. Just sit tight and do nothing. I'll talk with Oscar and we'll decide what needs to be done to bring this expanding cast of characters under control."

CHAPTER FORTY-TWO

*T*he *Times* office building was in its evening mode. The staff was much reduced, but the people working weren't going at a reduced pace.

"I'm glad we could meet in my office, Bob. With the time I'm putting in on the Sampson story, I'm finding it increasingly difficult to put in a regular workday. I need to spend extra hours here in the office to stay up to date on my other stories."

"I understand, Leslie. I'm the guy with time to spare and it's easy for me to forget you have more than one line in the water. You need to remind me about that from time to time."

"No problem for me, Bob. Let's use our time here to go over the news from my contact in pharmacology. As we suspected, the chemical being removed at York has properties that could make it valuable on the street. Since it's not a commercially available item there is no data on it from clinical studies." She paused and searched through the papers in a file she was holding.

"We're limited by the lack of direct testing trials, but the chemical bears some structural resemblance to a class of drugs called methamphetamines. These are psychostimulants that have actions in the brain. Our pharmacologist says there may be unreported data on the drug's chronic effect, but he is unaware of any. That's it."

"If that's all that's known, Leslie, why is someone so determined to keep its production secret? I guess that person knows something about it that we don't. The fact that it's worth killing for says a lot. Wait a minute. We're forgetting that Denise started down this road owing to a surprising record of low absenteeism in the crew producing the chemical. That suggests the work crew may have become chemically dependent on fumes and consequently drawn to work with greater than normal enthusiasm. The fact that it may also have led to nerve damage in at least two workers is the unfortunate coincidence that resulted in two women dying."

"Now what, Bob? We're up against another wall, but maybe a little farther ahead than the last time we hit one. The people who contracted to formulate the chemical are the critical link. They surely know about the chemical's potential as a street drug even though they may be unaware of its toxic potential. Trouble is they're guarding its production with other people's lives."

"Let's look at the contracts again and see who ordered the mother chemical. Then we'll have to figure out how to squeeze that person or entity to tell us who is responsible for the murders. I have copies of the contracts Eric and I scammed here in my briefcase. Let's take a look."

Bob and Leslie scanned the contracts and easily identified the parties who signed for Sampson and the customer, York Chemical. Larry Crandall had signed for Sampson and a barely legible Oscar Gleason had signed for York. Crandall was no surprise, but Gleason was a newcomer to their investigation.

"Leslie, I suggest we start with Crandall since Gleason is an unknown quantity and could prove dangerous. Since I've met Crandall on several occasions I'm willing to approach him to find out to what degree Sampson is involved in the dirty drug manufacture."

"I agree, Bob, but let's look a bit ahead. If Sampson is involved in the illegal business, are you suggesting Crandall had a hand in his own daughter's murder? That seems a far reach."

"I see your point, Les, but it's possible that Crandall only started the ball rolling and didn't have a hand in whatever happened after Sampson sent the product on to York. That might come out in my meeting with him. All we can do is ask questions and hope we don't stir up a hornets' nest."

"Do you meet with Crandall alone or do you want me with you?"

"I think he'll be less on guard in a one-on-one with a familiar face."

CHAPTER FORTY-THREE

Bob called and made an appointment with Larry Crandall. He was deliberately vague when Larry asked what they were meeting about. Nevertheless, Larry agreed to meet and suggested they use his home office as the informal meeting ground. Bob readily accepted and was now standing in front of the outer door of the house he and Denise had entered with such enthusiasm just months before.

Larry welcomed him inside and ushered him into what was obviously his workspace. The room was comfortably furnished with a dark wood desk and several brown leather upholstered armchairs. The bookcases were packed tight and most of the titles were books related to chemistry and pharmacology.

Bob tried to recall what Larry looked like when he visited several months ago. He was rather gaunt now with a clean-shaven face heavily lined with wrinkles. His hair, in need of cutting, was gray. He wore navy corduroy slacks with a plaid flannel shirt. He appeared a bit unkempt.

After exchanging a few pleasantries, Larry commented on how happy their gathering had been that evening Bob and Denise had spent here. His sorrow was quite evident and Bob could only feel a similar sadness. As if in agreement, they both put that mood behind them.

Larry asked the obvious question, "Okay, Bob it's your dime. What brings you here?"

For all the forethought he'd put into how he was going to handle the subject of this interview, Bob now just let it all hang out.

"Larry, I have some touchy matters to discuss with you. I'm not sure how deep your involvement is in them so I'll just have to trust my instincts."

"I'm a big boy, Bob. I can handle whatever you're going to dish out."

"Okay Larry, here goes. I have good reason to believe Sampson is involved in illegal drug trafficking. Denise innocently got involved in a tangential matter related to the product in question. She was considered a threat to the operation and was eliminated. That story about a rape gone bad in the park doesn't hold up. That same day her best friend, Chris Dinsmore, disappeared. The two women were murdered to keep the illegal operation in your facility safe from OSHA inspection. You signed a contract with a company called York Chemical to produce a product that York subsequently modifies to harvest a drug for illegal street consumption. That's what I know. What I don't know is who gave the order to eliminate Denise."

Larry sat in silence. Was this the moment of truth when he's called to account for his actions? This young man sitting opposite him had figured out the scheme he'd invented and put into operation. His own involvement, beyond creating and launching the system, was minimal.

Now he knew that Oscar had arranged his daughter's murder. The "corrective action" Oscar had alluded to when they met in Denver included the murder of Denise. Oscar may not have known the identity of the women eliminated or he would never have mentioned the "corrective action." He decided to offer little corroboration to Bob at this time. He wanted to consider his own options.

"Bob, please trust me. I had nothing to do with Denise's death. Nothing has caused me more heartache. I loved my daughter as much as any father ever loved a daughter and her loss pains me terribly every day."

"I accept that, Larry, but it was the Sampson process that put her life in jeopardy and ultimately claimed it."

"I'm not prepared to discuss the chemical processes you allude to, Bob. All you'll get from me tonight is my absolute denial of any involvement in my daughter's death. Now, why don't you just leave and let me consider my options in view of your clever detective work? Our meeting is over."

Larry rose and walked to the office door. He opened it and pointed to the front door of the house. Bob left without saying another word.

Sitting in his rented car, Bob began putting together what he'd learned tonight. The killing end of the operation had to reside at York, but the information York was making use of had to come from Sampson. The missing link could only be Mitch Trent. He was feeding York crucial information. He undoubtedly knew the people at York, and so it followed he'd have a good idea who was responsible for the murders.

CHAPTER FORTY-FOUR

Manny had a team of men from York stake out *The New York Times* building where Leslie worked. Although they saw her exit every day, she would get into a waiting cab or Uber, and they were unable to follow her to a final destination. Sometimes they even lost her in Brooklyn or Queens. They saw a man seated in the back of the vehicle she got into each time, but that was the extent of the information they reported to a very frustrated Manny Rufalo.

Manny decided on a change of plan. One of his men would enter the cab or Uber right behind Leslie, pushing her into the waiting man. With his gun drawn, the intruder would commandeer the car and direct the driver to take them to an address in the South Bronx where Oscar had friends who maintained a secure apartment in a rundown, partly deserted tenement.

This was accomplished with relative ease. The stranger in the backseat was told to get out in upper Manhattan, a significant distance from where the car took Leslie.

She was very frightened but struggled successfully to maintain her composure. Leslie hadn't realized she was this close to a violent end. Bob had warned her, but she wasn't about to slow down in pursuit of such a big story. She guessed her abduction was related to her visit to Sampson and the ride she had taken in the van to York. She tried to conjure up some information that would satisfy her kidnappers and allow her to remain alive. Leah had not survived her visit from these men.

Inside the apartment, Leslie, followed by the gunman from the car, was directed into a small living room with two frayed easy chairs and a sofa. A faded, framed poster of a painting by Monet was the only wall hanging. There was no window in this room. A partly disintegrated oriental rug covered most of the floor. The apartment smelled from a mixture of cooking odors, cigarettes, and disinfectant. Leslie sat on the sofa as she was directed.

She was fearful but determined to show no sign of her fear. She held her shoulder bag close against her side and somewhat behind her so it would be as inconspicuous as possible. So far no one had laid a hand on her, searched her, or spoken in a threatening manner.

A second man entered the room and, to her surprise, Leslie faintly recognized him. She wasn't sure where she'd met him, but he was clearly familiar. He was a dark-skinned, muscular guy of average height with black hair and a moustache. She tried to place him but had no success. As soon as he spoke, though, she recalled the rooftop party and the guy introduced by Tony Mason as a bowling teammate. His name was not coming through to her.

"Hello, Ms. Nugent. I'm glad you could come," Manny said with a slight smile. "All I want is some information. We can make this short and sweet if you'll just answer a few questions for me." Manny was trying very hard not to be threatening. Following Oscar's advice, he did not want this to end violently.

Manny paused and gave Leslie a moment to consider what he said. He was poker-faced and gave no indication that the alternative to cooperation would be a fate similar to Leah's.

"Okay. Tell me why you were out at Sampson last week."

Leslie decided to go with the truth even if it would be an abridged version. She wanted to get out of the apartment alive and didn't know how close she was to the edge of a precipice.

"I'm a reporter so I work on stories. I was following a hunch that Sampson might be making illegal drugs and shipping them to York. I wanted a sample of the material being shipped to York so I hitched a ride and drew a sample when the driver left me alone in the van. Can I go now?"

The man behind her placed a firm restraining hand on her shoulder that kept her from standing up.

"Not quite yet. What did you do with the sample?"

"I sent it for analysis. It didn't turn out to be a recognized street drug. End of story." Leslie hoped she could hold back enough and still satisfy this guy.

Manny wasn't going whole hog for the story. "What made you think illegal drugs were being shipped to York?"

Leslie had hoped she could avoid this question. "A policeman friend of mine works in the Drug Control section of the NYPD and he said an ongoing investigation was pointing in that direction. He didn't offer any details."

"So that's the whole story? I'm not sure you're being totally honest with me but I'll let it go for now. If there's more to the story than you just gave me we'll meet again. I'm not as gentle when I think I've been conned."

Leslie slid a hand into her shoulder bag and was prepared to go for her gun if this gentle parting was just smoke to cover a brutal ending. Without being asked she got up to leave. The restraining hand was removed from her shoulder.

"My man will drop you off wherever you want to go. No charge, Ms. Nugent. We're a very friendly organization when we're treated with respect. Your answer seemed pretty straightforward, so I'll take that for respect. I hope I won't be disappointed."

Leslie walked out slowly into the street, followed by the gunman who had delivered her to the apartment. She got into a waiting car and gave the driver an address where she wished to be delivered. They drove away as if nothing out of the ordinary had transpired.

Leslie hadn't lost her bladder content. That was a surprise. She'd feared that her fate would match Leah's. Giving a reasonable answer to the questions put to her was probably lifesaving. On the other hand, Leah had given them Leslie's name and still paid with her life.

"Manny." Now his name came back. She was glad she hadn't known it earlier and let him know that she'd recognized him.

CHAPTER FORTY-FIVE

Oscar and Manny were considering another "corrective action." Manny, as usual, was doing most of the talking and Oscar was listening very intently.

"Seems to me that Mitch is the connection between us and Sampson. He feeds us good info, but that info is what makes him a serious liability. I think it's time to sever that connection. The guys trying to figure out who is responsible for the loss of their sweeties will have a hard time getting to us unless Mitch leads them here. He's dangerous. At a minimum he needs a warning to keep us out of any discussion with those snooping guys, but I'm not sure that buys us the distance we need from all that's happened."

"Sounds like you want to go further, Manny. I'm afraid another killing connected to Sampson will make the police suspicious that something big is going down. On the other hand, we can't afford to leave him out there as a wildcard. He definitely knows too much and I bet the two guys trying to figure out what happened to their women will settle on him as having some part in the killings and the drug scheme."

"You're only making my case stronger for taking him out, Oscar. The only issue is how to do it and have it look like an accident with no back trail to Sampson. Remember that drunk driving death we arranged a few years ago? That worked out pretty good.

"I arrange to meet him at a bar and grill not far from your house and have a few drinks. I tell him you want to meet him at your house. I make it sound like he's being brought into the club. We drink some more and leave. Mike Sanchez is hiding in Mitch's car. We overpower him and put him out with chloroform. Some more booze is carefully poured down his throat and then Mike drives the car to some place where there's a big drop if you miss the turn. Mitch is placed in the driver's seat and the car goes into the ravine. That's it."

"Okay, Manny. I guess you got this figured. I agree he has to go. It's your game now. Just play it like you said."

Mitch took the call on his cell. Manny was upbeat and had good news. Oscar decided that Mitch had earned his place on the team and wanted to meet him tomorrow night. First, he and Manny would meet for drinks, and then the two of them would go on to Oscar's house for the introduction. They set a time and place. Manny offered his congratulations.

Mitch took a moment to reflect. Sure this was good news. They were pleased with the information he passed on to them and had always shown their appreciation. But this was unexpected. He reflected further. *I'm also the guy who could sink the whole operation. Does bringing me inside make me any less of a potential danger?* He didn't think so. Then why all this backslapping good news? He didn't want to look a gift horse in the mouth, but something didn't smell quite right. *Maybe they're setting me up for a big fall.* Just to play it safe he'd go along with the plans, but he'd carry a weapon in case the happy occasion turned sour.

CHAPTER FORTY-SIX

The pastry selection at Zabar's was awesome. Bob selected half a dozen to go along with the three large coffees he bought. Detective Gomes was happy to receive guests bearing such largesse.

"I guess you know the way to a cop's heart is through coffee and pastry. Many thanks, Bob. I've met Miss Nugent. Thank you, too."

"Detective, Leslie and I are feeling a bit too close to the murders for our own comfort. We didn't come to see you asking for protection. There's good reason to think that the murders emanate from York Chemical in Yonkers. We have reason to believe the two women were murdered because they knew two men at Sampson suffered nerve damage working on a new product and wanted OSHA called in. That would end profitable drug production."

Bob was sure they were on the right track, but was having trouble getting Gomes to partner up with them.

"We know Yonkers is not your jurisdiction, but two unsolved murders took place on your turf here in Manhattan. Maybe three, now that we know about Leah Rosen's murder. We need your help in getting to the killers."

"Look guys, the usual first step is finding evidence linking the suspected murderer to the crime," advised Detective Gomes. "The key word here is 'suspected.' There's gotta be good reason to think you've identified a good suspect. Then you can start planning on how you're going to tie him or her to the crime. Believe me, the police are very interested in solving the Crandall murder and the Dinsmore disappearance. We just haven't been able to tie anyone to the crimes."

Bob responded, "That's why we're sitting here, Detective. We need you to help us nail down a suspect. We don't have any contacts at York who could give us a place to start."

"You'd have to get familiar with York management and see if any likely suspects stand out. Then you may have to approach someone at York and see if your suspicions gain traction. Trouble is that could prove dangerous if your suspicions are accurate or at least threatening. I don't recommend that you do anything like that."

Bob and Leslie were listening intently. Each was independently trying to imagine an approach that would start that ball rolling. York was a blank slate at present. They needed to bring it out into the open.

"I wouldn't be surprised if Larry Crandall, the Sampson CEO, wants to find the person responsible for his daughter's death as much as all of us do. He must know the York organization pretty well. I wonder if he could be convinced to help out here." This was Bob's wishful thinking.

"Sounds like a good first step," was all the encouragement Gomes could offer.

CHAPTER FORTY-SEVEN

Old tenements in the South Bronx never were a comfortable area to work in, day or night. Too many alleys, seemingly deserted buildings, burnt out automobiles and trash strewn about. Chan Young always felt there were eyes on him even though the place was devoid of visible living bodies. It seemed deserted, but that was not the case. Drugs were prevalent and so were the users and purveyors. They just knew how to stay out of view. It was like a jungle where the animals knew how to stay invisible while being close at hand.

Chan was one of the prey animals in this jungle. Twelve years in the Drug Division of the NYPD had brought him to the South Bronx on a great many searches. He was dressed for the neighborhood he was visiting, wearing dark chinos, a blue chambray work shirt, and rumpled brown corduroy sport jacket. Chan was a six-footer with greying hair, loosely combed without a part. His face sported a grungy look, several days without a shave. Today he was looking for a user named Edgar Diaz. Eddie wasn't a snitch but he knew the drug scene here better than any cop could hope to. Chan used him as an extension of his own information base. Eddie was on Chan's regular payroll as a source of information, not as an informer. That distinction had kept him alive, although Chan wouldn't have been surprised to learn of his violent death on any given day.

Finding Eddie was a challenge. Somehow he would materialize out of the tenements to claim his pay. All Chan had to do was let his presence be known around the area by walking the streets. Sure enough, Eddie was walking toward him. He must have emerged from one of the boarded-up tenements just ahead on his left. Chan reached into his jacket inside pocket and held the folded envelope in his hand, showing just enough for Eddie to see that today was payday.

"Hey, Eddie. How's it goin'?"

They casually wandered over to the stoop in front of a three-story house and sat next to each other on the lower steps. The envelope in Chan's hand was casually placed in one of the planter pots on the steps. Eddie took note.

"Things are going just fine, Chan. Is there anything I can do for you?"

"I'm just on a general tour of the neighborhood, Eddie, but I'm all ears if there's anything you think I should know about."

"Well, there is something you might like to look into. I don't know what it means, but it is strange. Several guys and one woman in the 'hood have come down with a leg problem. It's mostly a loss of feeling in the feet that makes walking a bit unsteady for them. I mention it because it's new in the area. They're all users so there's some concern that the street dust could be the cause. That would be bad for business, so the concern affects customers and sellers. Just thought you ought to know."

"Thanks, Eddie. That's the kind of info I'm lookin' for from you. Do you happen to know the names of any of these poor souls? I'd like to ask them a few questions."

"You know my rules, Chan. No names. Just general info. Helps keep me breathing."

"Okay, Eddie. I understand. Tell me, has there been any change in the street dust? Any new product? Any new dust added to the old? Anything to help me understand what's behind these leg problems."

"Well, I think some new product came to the street several months ago and has been spread around quite a bit. I'm not a dealer so I don't know any details, but I bet one of the dealing guys could provide some of that info. You know some dealers. Ask them. I gotta go. Good luck, Chan."

Eddie walked away and quickly melted into the brick jungle all around them. The envelope in the planter had somehow left with him. Chan was left to ponder how to deal with the new information Eddie had put in his hands. He decided it might be a useful lead to a new drug supplier.

The next step would be to see if this leg problem was more pervasive than just the three cases Eddie knew about. To find out, he'd put a notice in the recently circulated newsletter for NYPD. The newsletter was sent out to all members of the force and was considered a worthwhile innovation by the new Chief of Police. It was sent out as an email and reached every officer's computer and cellphone. He would be asking if anyone had seen or heard of any experience recently that was similar to Eddie's.

Sometimes things *do* work as they're supposed to. Claudia Gomes was reading the newsletter on her cellphone as she sipped her morning coffee. Chan Young's note struck a chord. Her two amateur detectives had cited a similar experience with possible nerve damage in two Sampson workers. It seemed too much of a coincidence, especially since the two independent reports seemed to tie back to drugs. She punched in Young's cellphone number.

CHAPTER FORTY-EIGHT

Leslie was way ahead of Claudia Gomes. When Chan told her about the possible nerve-damaged users she immediately sensed a killer story. She thought back to the rooftop party where she'd met two users with possible nerve problems in their feet. She'd filed that away but didn't bury it. Now it was screaming at her. This story was getting bigger by the moment.

Her plan was to not rely on only street addicts, but rather seek out middle class and higher adults who were victimized by the toxic product. In this way she might have a larger number of different connections to trace back to the source.

Resourceful and tireless, Leslie obtained a list of board-certified neurologists from the New York City Medical Society. She and two student interns at the paper began calling doctors and, using a prepared text, sought to determine if there was an uptick in the number of patients who had presented with recent onset of leg symptoms or "peripheral neuropathy" as the doctors referred to it. Doctors would be reluctant to reveal names but, if the numbers were suggestive of a toxic basis for the neuropathies, the doctors might be willing to probe their patients about their drug usage. It was a touchy matter.

It didn't take long to confirm that neuropathies had significantly increased in frequency and that patients were willing to confess to drug usage if there was a chance that this knowledge could help cure their condition.

When Chan told Leslie the gist of his conversation with Claudia Gomes, her excitement level could not be contained. Not only was she on to a drug story of great importance, but there was a murder story thrown in for good measure. She had no idea what Sampson Industries was all about, but finding out was now her first order of business. She'd visit the business and read any articles about it in *the Times'* archives.

Demonstrating that some relatively well-off users were suffering from the same nerve damage being experienced by the street addict population gave her story greater reach than a tragedy confined to lower class users. The two rooftop sufferers were not street addicts. It would be up to the drug police to determine if a single source of drug could be creating the problem.

She called Bob and alerted him to the forward movement on the toxic drug matter. Her postulated scenario was readily agreed to by him. The Sampson workers and the drug users were likely injured by the same neurotoxic chemical. The workers were inadvertent "users," probably through fumes where the chemical was in production. The users were injured the old-fashioned way; they purposefully introduced the chemical into their bodies, unaware that they were poisoning their nervous systems.

Leslie's story was still consigned to the back pages in the Metro section of *The Times*. She couldn't identify the drug source with certainty at this stage. She also didn't have enough evidence to tie in the murders. Nevertheless, her competition was barely visible in the rearview mirror.

CHAPTER FORTY-NINE

Bob was back in the Crandall home for a second try at enlisting Larry in the quest to identify Denise's killer. Larry had been reluctant to meet again, but on reflection he saw Bob as a potential instrument to gain a measure of revenge for Denise's death. He and Bob were on the same path with the same goal, but Larry had a bigger agenda. Once Oscar was eliminated, he'd convince the higher-ups in the larger organization to install him as the head of the Sampson-York enterprise with a commitment to keeping the goals of the partnership the same as they were before. After all, he had brought Sampson into their orbit and worked flawlessly with Oscar. He could be trusted. His neck was already stuck out, so there was no safe exit for him.

He decided to help Bob Hillman and in the process kill two birds with one stone: vengeance for Denise's death and expansion of his original plan to its logical completion.

He greeted Bob with some feigned reluctance. He'd decided that his help would be provided, but without the enthusiasm he harbored within. They retreated into the library where they met the previous time. They settled into two comfortable easy chairs that flanked a small table.

"Over the phone you indicated that you were looking for information about the York organization. You carefully avoided telling me why you wanted the information. So, spell it out for me."

"Okay, Larry. I've been over the facts surrounding Denise's death and, coupled with your seemingly sincere claim of innocence, I'm left with the conclusion that people at York Chemical were behind the killing. The motive is clear enough. Now I need to put some names on the organization and see if a logical suspect emerges. That's where you come in."

"York is our major client. I don't want to see that relationship go down the drain because of some vengeful accusation that has no firm foundation. I'll only go just so far in helping you until you've made a good case against some individual or group of individuals."

"Fair enough, Larry. I can work within those boundaries. It does me no good to swing wildly and probably miss the real culprit."

"Okay, as long as we both understand each other. York is a very small organization. Oscar Gleason is the president and his associate, Manny Rufalo, is his close advisor and the 'fixer,' if I may use an old-fashioned term. Manny is dangerous so don't cross him. There are no other officers but there are a number of foot soldiers who carry out orders from the top. Oscar and I have gotten along very well, each recognizing the other's turf. That's all I can tell you, Bob."

"Thanks, Larry. That is helpful. I understand your reluctance to damage a working relationship. I can only assure you that I'm not diving in here before carefully weighing the evidence I uncover. With that assurance, I'll take leave of you. I can find my way out."

Larry sat back in his comfortable chair. He'd put the finger on Oscar without accusing him of anything. Now, he hoped Bob was as good at closing this case as he had been at unraveling the drug production story.

CHAPTER FIFTY

B ob discussed his strategy with Leslie. Following Lieutenant Gomes's advice, he felt he now had a good suspect for Denise's killing. Oscar Gleason and Manny Rufalo were the likely killers. Now he needed evidence. The two of them were not going to confess, but their source of information might be more vulnerable. That would be Mitch Trent. Manny Rufalo was Bob's person of interest because Larry had labeled him the "fixer." He would likely have had a hand in any violent acts attributed to York.

Bob's plan was to get Trent in an isolated setting and squeeze him to give up the men he fed information to that led to the killings. He was determined to make him talk. Use of force was out of character for him, but his anger level was peaking. He'd do what was necessary.

He'd stalk Trent until he saw an opportunity to catch him alone. His vantage point was a parking lot of a small factory adjacent to Sampson.

On his first day, observing from 4:00 p.m., he saw Trent leave work after five and drive straight home. By nine he hadn't left his house so Bob called it a day. An unrevealing day.

On his second day, Trent again left work around five and drove home. This time he emerged at seven thirty and drove away in his car.

He drove to a bar and grill about thirty minutes away, parked in the adjacent, dimly lit parking area, and entered alone. Bob parked in the same lot as Trent but some distance away. Not ten minutes later a man fitting Manny Rufalo's description pulled into the one available parking space in front of the restaurant and went inside. Another man stayed behind in the car.

Bob assumed Trent and Manny Rufalo were conducting some sort of business inside. It surely was no coincidence that the two of them had arrived within minutes of each other at this particular bar and grill. The York "fixer" and Sampson's COO were not a likely business twosome.

Out of the corner of his eye, Bob saw the man in Manny's car get out and go over to Trent's car. Strangely, he got into the back seat. The parking area was poorly lit so Bob's view of the cars was limited. This whole drama playing out before him was curious, to say the least.

Less than an hour later the front door to the bar and grill opened and out came a smiling Mitch Trent and Manny Rufalo. They had been inside long enough to have a few drinks but not long enough for dinner. They split and headed to their respective cars. Manny stood alongside his car in front of the restaurant, watching Trent get into his car in the side parking area. Bob was now focused on Trent's car and had a sense of foreboding. He instinctively reached into his glove compartment and drew out the handgun Eric had been able to purchase. Something was going down and it didn't look good for Mitch Trent.

Bob left his car and saw Manny heading to Mitch's car just as he was. Manny was unaware of Bob's presence until they converged some thirty feet from Mitch's car.

"Stay away from that car, Manny," was Bob's forceful command.

"Who the hell are you, Mack?" was Manny's response without even looking at Bob.

"Stand away from the car and don't make a move for your gun. I have you covered and now I'm going to open the car door. Don't be foolish."

Bob opened the car door and Mitch sprawled out onto the parking lot concrete. The man in the back seat opened the opposite side door and raced into the darkened back area of the parking lot.

"Mitch, are you alright? Can you hear me?" Bob implored the immobile figure of Mitch Trent. "Why don't you just leave, Manny, I'm going to attend to Mitch. I know where to find you."

"You should have minded your own business, whoever you are. We'll meet again and I don't think you'll enjoy the reunion." Manny turned and walked slowly to his car.

Bob kept his eyes on Manny and saw the man who ran away return to Manny's side and get into the car with him. They drove away.

Mitch was groaning and coughing. Bob took this as a good sign and let him lie on his side with his jacket rolled up under his head. He gradually returned to near normal control and allowed Bob to help seat him in his own car on the passenger side.

"I'm sure glad you were here. Why the hell were you, by the way? You saved my life so I guess I shouldn't ask a lot of questions," Mitch croaked in a very hoarse voice.

"We'll have a lot to talk about when I get you to your house. In the meantime, rest your voice. I'm sure your voice box was bruised during the attempt to strangle you unconscious or dead. Your friend, Manny, left without saying goodbye." Bob did a quick assessment of Mitch's condition and felt he was almost back to normal. "Now, I'll drive you home. You can pick up your car tomorrow.

CHAPTER FIFTY-ONE

"Amazing!" was Chan Young's response to the large number of email responses to his call for any users with new neurological problems. A number described mild gait disorders but a few were more serious. Now the call from Claudia Gomes seemed to seal the deal. Next he needed to cull these cases and see if the drug source could be identified. This was not always so simple since the street vendors were reluctant to turn snitch for a variety of reasons, including self-preservation, but also because they had very little information about upstream sources. Armed with Claudia's information they had a good idea where some, or all, of the drug may have originated. They could bypass the dealers and go right to the source.

Claudia Gomes and Chan Young were meeting for the first time. Sitting in her office in the Homicide Department's Manhattan headquarters, they traded stories about how each had acquired the information about drug exposure and possible nerve damage. Chan and Claudia were both surprised at how well their stories meshed.

"We're so jaded on bad leads, Claudia, that we're stunned when something works out and makes sense. We're both beholden to people outside the force who pointed us in the right directions. My reporter friend and your informant who lost his close friend were key people who helped put this case together."

Chan stopped talking for a moment while they both considered how the crucial information came to their attention.

"Claudia, I think we're really on to something here. I received a number of calls from detectives with similar drug information. In your case, Claudia, there's good reason to believe your murders are all tied back to the drugs in an effort to prevent discovery of the source."

"I guess my civilian helpers did solid spade work, Chan, and I failed to give them any real assistance. I feel lousy about that. Now I want to assure their safety after foolishly sending them out to gather more evidence."

"Our drug force is out trying to trace the drugs used by the injured users. The two Sampson workers are pointing us at the likely source. I'm sure when our drug investigators are given your information it will point them to the same source. In the meantime, Hillman and Nugent should retreat to a safe haven. Then we need to pick up the trail and do the police job they laid open for us, Claudia."

"We also need to get the Yonkers police in on the case. It would appear that the drug source is on their turf. Our two forces need to work jointly on this. I'm sure you agree, Chan. I'm heading up to the home of Mitch Trent, a senior management guy at Sampson who may have some useful information about the decisions made by that organization. Should prove interesting."

At her end, Gomes now realized how close to real danger she had placed two zealous citizens when she encouraged them to dig into the organization that might be responsible for the three murders on her turf. She punched in Bob Hillman's number on her cell.

239

CHAPTER FIFTY-TWO

Brenda Trent greeted Mitch and Bob at the door. She and Bob helped Mitch into the house and lay him down on the living room sofa. Bob helped her calm down after he gave her a truncated version of the evening's events. Mitch raised himself up on his elbows and introduced Bob to his wife.

"Brenda, this guy literally saved my life. I barely know him but I know I owe him big. What a night! I was such a dupe. I thought I was on my way to a big thank you meeting but it turned out to be an execution."

"Lay back and relax, Honey. There'll be time to talk later. Rest is what you need now."

Mitch rolled onto his side facing the back of the sofa and was asleep in less than a minute. Brenda threw an afghan cover over him, then she and Bob retreated to the kitchen.

Bob's phone rang. Seeing Claudia Gomes's name on the screen, he was quick to answer the call.

"Bob Hillman here. I see your name on the screen Lieutenant."

"I'm calling for several reasons, Mr. Hillman. Chan Young from the NYPD Drug Taskforce has found evidence of more nerve damage among users that meshes nicely with the information you passed on to me about the reason for the murder of Denise Crandall and probable murder of Chris Dinsmore. He and I, in conjunction with the Yonkers police, are assembling the necessary documents to initiate searches and serve subpoenas."

"Well, I have some news for you. Just tonight there was an attempt on the life of Mitch Trent. I think he knows a lot about what's been going on at Sampson and York and was scheduled to be shut up tonight. I'm at his house now waiting for him to wake up from a deep sleep. You should be here. I'm sure he'll have a lot to say that will clear up much of the mystery surrounding the killings."

"Thanks for the invitation. I'll take you up on it. Give me Trent's address. I should get free shortly. Please be careful, Mr. Hillman. There's a lot of violence involved in this case. Don't let yourself be fed into it."

Bob filled her in on the attack on Mitch. Again, Gomes advised him to keep a safe distance from the whole drug-murder cascade. She and the Yonkers police would come to the Trent house and take over. She'd be there in little over an hour.

Bob reluctantly agreed to hold off on questioning Mitch until she arrived.

Brenda picked up where she and Bob had left off when he took the call.

"I have no idea what's going on, Bob. Mitch and I talk very little about his work. As a matter of fact we talk very little about anything."

"If it's any comfort, I'm a bit in the dark about his work as well. I do need to talk to him though, to better understand the background of tonight's assault. I'm sure the attempt on his life is connected to what

I'm looking for. I think he has some very useful information regarding Sampson and the death of Denise Crandall. Her murder is the reason I was in the vicinity and able to intercede when Mitch was attacked."

"You knew Denise? Mitch was like a close uncle to her. He took her death hard. I still can't believe she's gone. But what does Mitch have to do with her death?"

"Brenda, there are some unsavory things happening in and around Sampson that I'm trying to understand. Mitch, I think, holds the key to much of it. I'm sorry if I'm bringing unwelcome news into your house. I really mean that. Why don't we leave it at that for now? I'll just wait here until Mitch wakes up. The police are on their way here. They'll also be very interested in what he has to say."

"Seeing as how you saved his life, I think you're entitled to what-ever you need in this house. I'll make some coffee for you. Just go into the living room and make yourself comfortable."

CHAPTER FIFTY-THREE

Oscar took the news from Manny over the phone with his usual placid demeanor. Inside he was seething. For some reason they were unable to shake free of the inquisitive outsiders. Now, one of them had interfered in a carefully planned elimination. This had to stop.

"So Manny, did you recognize the good Samaritan who saved Mitch?"

"No, I didn't, but he knew Mitch. Referred to him by name. He knew my name too. He was also armed. It seemed he must have been watching what was going on. Who was he watching? Me? Mitch? This was no passerby stepping in to stop a crime."

"Well, Mitch is no longer our friendly source of inside information. Before we take him out we have to find out who his friend is.

Right now, though, I need some time alone to think this through." Manny got the message and left Oscar's office.

For now, Manny would have to take an extended leave until Oscar could figure out a way to eliminate Mitch. Now that Mitch would be on high alert he would be a more formidable target.

He also had a new player to worry about. If he was a close friend of Mitch he may be carrying around some information that they were trying very hard to keep to themselves. This new guy's angle was unclear to him, but he worried that Mitch might spill the beans to him, the very reason they had earmarked Mitch for disposal. The fact that this guy was at the scene of the botched attack made it highly likely that he was a player. But what was he after?

On a hunch Oscar made a phone call to Larry Crandall.

"This is a surprise, Oscar. I can't recall our last phone conversation. You must be after some important information. What is it you're looking for?"

"You know I wouldn't call you unless I needed your help in a touchy matter. I'm trying to identify a guy who seems to be very interested in the Sampson-York operation. He knew Mitch Trent and even knew Manny. He's obviously digging deep into our business. Do you know who I'm talking about?"

Larry hesitated a moment and tried to figure out if giving Bob's name to Oscar would come back to haunt him. He decided to take the chance.

"The guy is Bob Hillman. He was very close to my daughter and may be looking for a measure of revenge. Be careful. He's smart."

After hanging up, Larry wondered if Bob Hillman was going to get to Oscar and find his measure of revenge or if Oscar, using Manny, would take out Bob to save his drug business.

His daughter's death demanded payback and Bob Hillman was his only vehicle for achieving that.

CHAPTER FIFTY-FOUR

His home office was where he did his best thinking. Larry Crandall had thought his plan to use Sampson as a first step in getting a new drug to the street was clever. Using York to do the heavy lifting and running the risk was his way to distance himself from the dirty final product. Sooner or later Oscar would stumble and he, Larry Crandall, would inherit the whole operation. Not that he cared about ownership. Just coming out on top was enough for him. He never anticipated all the collateral damage.

The death of his daughter had been a shock. That was beyond the range of his imagination. Now Bob Hillman appears on the scene and seems to be putting all the pieces together. Sure he could be Larry's accidental fixer who wreaks vengeance on Oscar Gleason and his crew, but that would leave Bob as the guy carrying Larry's plan around.

His telephone rang. It was the Trent house calling. "Hello, this is Larry. What's up?"

"Larry, this is Brenda. I'm calling to tell you Mitch was attacked tonight and nearly killed. He would have been, if a fellow named Bob Hillman hadn't intervened. Bob is over here now waiting for Mitch to wake up so he can question him about the episode. He says there are some unsavory things taking place at Sampson and that Mitch may know quite a lot about what's going on. I called to let you know that the attack took place and to ask if you know what Bob Hillman is referring to."

"I'm as much in the dark as you are, Brenda. But I'm deeply concerned about what happened to Mitch tonight. I'm going to come over and hear Mitch's take on the attack. I know Bob Hillman. He's a good man and has been trying to find out the real facts surrounding Denise's death. They were very close so he's motivated to find the truth."

"I don't know how long Mitch'll be asleep, Larry. He was very worn out by the experience. That's a special kind of fatigue so it might be a matter of hours. You're welcome to do whatever you want. Come on over and have a cup of coffee with me."

"Thanks, Brenda. I'll be there in about an hour."

Larry wasn't sure how much Mitch knew about the drug scheme and the relationship with York, but he was confident that Mitch didn't know the depth of his relationship to Oscar Gleason. Mitch's role in Denise's death was something he wanted to hear firsthand.

It seemed to Larry that this was a good time to clean up the labs and eliminate all traces of the illicit chemicals. He made a call and ordered just such a cleanup ASAP. He then called Oscar to warn him to do the same. They would hunker down and ride out any searches that might be coming their way. Once the dust settled, they could resume business as usual. A few weeks off wouldn't hurt.

CHAPTER FIFTY-FIVE

Manny was still stewing over the way the evening had played out. On top of that, Oscar had dissed him very politely. The boss didn't realize how close they were to seeing the whole organization unravel. Mitch was still the same time bomb they had set out to kill, only now he had an armed ally and knew he was slated for disposal. The right course of action was to finish the job, killing Mitch and his buddy.

No one else knew about the earlier attack to the best of his knowledge. The killing in his house would be difficult for the police to explain. There was no obvious motive for the police to uncover. He and his men would remove the body of this interfering friend and drive away his car in order to keep the killing scene as simple as possible. At least he and Oscar had kept Mitch and his pipeline to them very secret.

Now he was sitting in his car outside Mitch's house along with two armed associates, deciding how to enter the house and do what was necessary. Oscar had not sanctioned this attack, but Manny was confident he would accept the action once he knew that the outcome was favorable. He respected Oscar's concern about drawing the attention of the police to their operation but his rage couldn't be contained.

His plan was a dramatic entry, avoiding any armed resistance. He would kill Mitch and his friend and not worry about any information that may have been passed between them. Dead is dead and the information dies with them. One man was sent to the back of the house to make a rear entrance. Manny and the other gunman would ring the doorbell and start firing as soon as the door was opened and they saw a live target.

As planned, they rang the bell, the door opened, and Manny shot Brenda before she could utter a word. He and a companion rapidly advanced inside, saw Mitch sitting up on a sofa with shocked surprise on his face. Manny put three bullets into his chest, sending him and the sofa over backward. The rear entry man entered through an unlocked back door as soon as he heard the gunfire. He was advancing through the kitchen when Bob shot him in the back of the head. Bob had been leaving the bathroom and had sought cover in the kitchen pantry after hearing the gunshots.

Manny and his companion now spread out, looking for the other intended victim. The second gunman found his partner lying face down in the hallway leading back to the kitchen. Bob could see the reflection of a man heading his way in the glass that covered a picture in the hallway. Trained in house-to-house combat in the marines, he knew how to act in just this situation. Without hesitation he spun out of the alcove in a crouch and fired several rounds into the advancing man. The second gunman didn't have time to get off a shot. He added to the body count in the narrow hallway. Bob quickly spun back into the protection of the alcove.

Manny's call to his associates went unanswered. He now knew he was on a solo mission. Neither he nor Bob was sure where the other was in the house. Manny considered his situation. He had lost the element of surprise along with his two soldiers. Mitch's friend was still alive, so the original objective had not been fully achieved. On the other hand there was the chance that Mitch had not passed along much of what he knew about the Sampson-York operation.

Bob believed that the remaining attacker had to be Manny, intent on finishing the job that Bob had interrupted earlier that evening. He had probably shot Mitch on the way in and was now hoping to finish him and seal off any information Mitch may have passed on to him.

Bob decided to go on the offensive. He gambled on Manny being nowhere near his two fallen soldiers, leaving Bob a clear path out the back door. He quickly made his exit and then, crouching low, made his way around the house to a spot behind some bushes near the attached garage. He waited.

Manny chose to retreat rather than make a dangerous effort to find his other target. He left the relative safety of the living room, stepped over the body of Brenda Trent in the hallway, and was out the front door in a few seconds. He was about to run to his car when Bob Hillman came out from behind a bush and told him to freeze. He chose to ignore the command and instead bolted for his car. Bob's first shot missed him, but a second hit his right shoulder. Manny hid behind his car in the street while Bob was unprotected on the front lawn. Manny's shooting arm was badly injured. Bob took advantage of Manny's injury to run to the safety of his car in the driveway. It was at this juncture that Larry Crandall's car pulled into the outer side of the driveway alongside Bob's car.

Manny was experienced at raids like this. He always had a back-up in case things didn't go his way. In this case the backup was lifesaving for him. A non-descript Toyota Corolla came up behind Manny. He stayed low, opened the back door and slid in. They quickly drove away.

Bob stood cursing in the driveway. In a full adrenaline rush, he hated to see Manny get away. Firefights like this in Afghanistan lasted minutes but seemed to last for hours. So had this one. It started with the attackers rushing in the front door and ended with one survivor of the attack team driving away wounded. It had lasted less than ten minutes and left four dead people in the house. Bob was exhausted and sat down on the front steps to the house.

Larry Crandall came out of his car. He'd come over to hear what Mitch was going to say. He'd had trepidation, but on learning from Bob that Mitch was dead, a great weight was lifted from his shoulders. He didn't know the full extent of what Mitch had known about the drug operation, but now it was moot and he was relieved.

"Was that Manny Rufalo you were shooting it out with, Bob?"

"Yeah, that was Manny. He and his friends killed Mitch and Brenda. He was the guy who set Mitch up for an attack earlier at a nearby bar and grill. Looks like he was trying to finish the job here. A very determined guy. I guess they didn't want Mitch carrying around a lot of information about their operation. This was how they planned to shut him up. It worked. I never got to hear Mitch out."

Bob stood up as a Yonkers police car pulled into the driveway, preventing any cars from leaving. He dropped his gun at his feet and stood silently as two uniformed officers approached. A long evening of explanation began.

CHAPTER FIFTY-SIX

The Trent house was crawling with cars when Claudia Gomes pulled up and found a place to park in the street. She identified herself to the uniformed policeman guarding the entranceway and was allowed inside. She was shocked to learn that Mitch Trent had been killed. In the dining room she saw Bob Hillman being questioned by a plainclothes woman whom she assumed to be a Yonkers homicide detective. She introduced herself to the detective and was given a faint smile by a rather worn Bob Hillman.

"I'm Lieutenant Claudia Gomes. NYC Homicide. I'm a friend of Mr. Hillman."

"Hello, Detective Gomes. I'm Lieutenant Annemarie Coleman, Yonkers Homicide. I've been questioning Mr. Hillman for about fifteen minutes. You're welcome to join us. He's weary but is being very cooperative. Seems there was a surprise attack on the house that left four bodies for us. Bob and one of the attackers were having a shootout on the lawn when the remaining attacker managed to slip away in a backup vehicle. He's been giving me a lot of background on the attack. I'm reeling from the complexity of the information leading up to this moment."

"I know a bit about the case and was coming here to learn what light one of the victims was going to shed on his role in the whole bloody mess. If you have four bodies here, I count at least seven total."

"Maybe you and I should sit down somewhere, Claudia, and you could fill me in. Bob here is suffering from battle fatigue compounded by very little sleep tonight. He should rest. I'll take his full statement later."

"Sounds good to me, Annemarie, let's find a quiet spot while one of your officers takes Bob upstairs to rest."

CHAPTER FIFTY-SEVEN

Manny filled in Oscar over the phone. Manny knew that he would have to go into hiding and not be seen anywhere near York Chemical. There was a physician they used at times like this, so that was where he was heading to have his shoulder wound cared for. Oscar spoke with Manny's backup driver and told him to return to York once Manny embarked on his escape route. They had planned for such a contingency so now Manny would be able to fade away and be impossible to find.

Chan Young had gathered sufficient evidence to justify the search warrant he needed to investigate the operation of York Chemical and Sampson Industries. The drug tracks from the users to the street sellers and finally to the source of the drug itself all led to York. Coupled with the two neuropathy cases emanating from Sampson, the evidence pointed to some kind of Sampson-York partnership at the root of it all.

Warrants were served and searches carried out. Neither suspect facility was tainted by illicit drugs. Larry Crandall and Oscar Gleason had taken the necessary precautions in their facilities. They'd covered their tracks even before Chan Young had completed his investigation of the cases of neuropathic damage (the term used by the neurologists at Columbia) that led to the Sampson-York facilities.

Chan knew they'd been too slow to catch the two criminal enterprises in the act. He knew who the guilty parties were, but there was no hard evidence. As he learned of the attack at the Trent house he believed that their best witness had been eliminated. His information must have been potentially very damaging to justify such a risky raid. He and Claudia agreed it was a good case, but their investigation would now have to await some serendipitous break to restore its momentum. They had other cases to pursue.

Bob Hillman accepted the news from Claudia Gomes with a wry smile. He knew they had missed by a whisker. Manny's bold blitzkrieg had done the job. It had silenced the one witness who could upend the illegal operation and explain the deaths of Denise and Chris.

Like the police, Leslie was left with a good story but no satisfying closure. Absent a corroborating witness, she had to work with some speculative conclusions. She'd just have to go with what she had.

BOOK THREE

CHAPTER ONE

S ampson and York were back in business. Oscar realized that they had survived a very close call, but with Mitch out of the way the road seemed clear. The one loose end was Mitch's buddy who had saved Mitch's neck originally and then turned back Manny's attack. Larry knew the "buddy" was Bob Hillman.

Neither Larry nor Oscar knew what, if anything, Mitch had revealed to Bob. Since Bob had made no waves, they assumed he hadn't been able to hear Mitch out before he was killed by Manny. They assumed Bob would now go back home to San Francisco. They were unaware of his relationship with Leslie Nugent and were not aware of the comprehensive newspaper piece on the drug saga that was soon to be in print.

Oscar felt badly about Manny. The latter had taken it on himself to finish Mitch. Now he was in hiding for a prolonged period. Oscar saw to it that money was made available to him through street connections. In any event, his unsanctioned action had removed the one person who could have sunk their ship.

The situation had returned to where it was before two women had innocently walked in on the drug manufacturing scheme.

Well, not exactly to where it had been. Elaine was suing Larry for divorce. Marge Cameron had given notice at Sampson.

CHAPTER TWO

Exponential growth of the alternative energy market was forcing Bob Hillman to expand his office staff and create an additional office site in Wyoming. He was being kept incredibly busy, but busy meant more profits, and more profits meant greater support for his education foundation. Busy also meant distraction from the mess he'd been involved with back East. Leslie had begun to brighten his outlook on the future. She hadn't placed any demands on him. They continued along with a growing sense that something good was going to happen if they stayed on their current course. He was closing the book on the Sampson-Denise affair.

CHAPTER THREE

O scar decided on an aggressive approach to protect his interests. Larry Crandall had identified the guy who was making
waves, the guy who initially saved Mitch Trent, the guy who
seemed to be attached to the deceased Crandall woman and the guy who
shot Manny. The guy was a potential menace to Oscar's interests.

Stepping out of character, Oscar decided on a preventative elimination, but it would take place on the guy's home turf, three thousand
miles away from York. That distance would help keep any suspicion away
from Yonkers and York Chemical. He would get word to Manny that he
had a job for him. Manny was a wanted man, but his disappearance was a
total success. The police were unable to locate him. He was able to ma-
neuver with relative freedom in the San Francisco area. By being patient,
Oscar had allowed this scheme to hatch in an ideal manner.

He didn't want to jeopardize Manny so they met at a hotel near Tulsa's airport. They discussed several options but soon realized that there was no need for a complex plan. Manny would observe Hillman for a while and then decide on a quick assassination. It would go down as a murder with no clear suspect and no clear motive. Oscar left the details up to Manny and departed Tulsa, feeling he had made an important move that would clean up a dangling loose end.

CHAPTER FOUR

Hunting season was well underway in upstate New York. Danny Higgins and his golden lab, Esquire, were plowing through some dense underbrush in search of a suitable deer for killing. Esquire started to dig up a patch of dirt just to the left of the path they were trying to follow. Danny could not persuade her to let it go. Her determination was fierce. He decided to give in to her instincts and use the pause to rest against a tree.

The long object in Esquire's mouth was covered in dirt, but was definitely a long bone. Could be a bear's or a deer's, but on closer inspection it clearly was human. Esquire soon unearthed another. He stopped her digging, tied her to a tree, and called the local forest ranger on his phone.

Two hours later the ranger and two men with shovels and other gear found the hunter and set out to excavate the burial site. It was indeed a human's remains, about a year old. They trucked their findings back to the police station and turned them over to the authorities. The burial site offered no identification material. The medical examiner concluded that the body was that of a woman about forty years old. The cause of death was a gunshot to the head. The weapon was probably a small caliber handgun. One shot had done the deed. There was an entrance wound in the skull but no exit wound. Sure enough, a single, much damaged bullet was found in the cranial vault.

State Police searched their file for missing women aged thirty to forty-five who were missing approximately one year. This woman's teeth were in excellent repair, so they focused on women from middle class or greater means. Just playing the odds, they first concentrated on married women. DNA was sent for analysis but would take a few weeks.

New York police had a few possible hits, but liked a missing thirty-nine year old married doctor who had vanished without any reason. They requested the dental x-rays of the corpse and compared them with dental x-rays of the missing doctor. The match was perfect. Chris Dinsmore's disappearance was no longer a mystery.

Claudia Gomes called Eric Dinsmore at work and told him about the body's discovery in upstate New York. Eric was not surprised, but was still saddened to learn the outcome he'd feared had come to pass. When he hung up the phone he was in tears, not for himself, but for Chris and how her life had ended so senselessly. Later that night he called Bob Hillman to close that loop.

CHAPTER FIVE

Eric Dinsmore was caught in a twisted plot. In his private life he was deeply involved in the York matter, working with Bob Hillman to avenge the killing of his wife. In recent weeks he had made himself less available to work alongside Bob. He claimed the demands of his practice had mounted up and needed his personal attention. In his practice life, that same drug cover-up confronted him from a totally different angle. He was dependent on Alyssa Ross for his livelihood. As her "fixer" he carried out many unsavory tasks for her in addition to serving as her close personal attorney for many legitimate matters. Although Ross-Wagner employed a team of attorneys at a prestigious Wall Street law firm, Eric was the attorney who coordinated legal matters.

There was no problem feeding Alyssa the information she was seeking about the problem in Yonkers. This was delivered to her in person in her Manhattan office. He gave her a pretty complete picture of the troublesome matter.

He and Alyssa avoided emails and informational phone calls. He had to swear that no written memos would be in his files. They worked on a handshake basis and had to trust each other.

The information from Eric told a story of deception and cover-up that had grown increasingly complex and taken more lives than expected. A vengeful killer, close to the York president, was on the loose and might carry out more killings. Alyssa sized up the situation and, with Eric's concurrence, decided to eliminate the killer and hopefully restore peace to the troubled situation. This was Eric's task.

Using no names he quickly contacted Oscar Gleason in the name of the organization and was informed that Manny Rufalo was in San Francisco. This struck him as more than coincidence since Bob Hillman was a potential target. Eric contacted his West Coast counterpart and passed along the request from Alyssa. The timing was crucial.

CHAPTER SIX

San Francisco provided plenty of cover for Manny. Using a new name and documents provided by Oscar and the organization, he was all but invisible. His shoulder wound had healed well, but memory of the shooter still rankled him. He was determined to finish the job he'd started that night at the Trent house.

Oscar initially was angry that Manny had acted on his own after the initial attempt on Mitch's life failed, but he soon mellowed on the subject when he saw no serious fallout from the second attack that day. In fact, the elimination of Mitch Trent had been a decisive move.

As Oscar suggested, Manny had begun surveillance of Bob at his San Francisco home and office. Once he could predict Bob's coming and going moves, he'd be ready to pounce and end this guy's life. This would erase a potentially dangerous witness for York and also erase his own night of failure from his personal memory.

He was well-concealed in the dark, standing behind some tall rhododendron bushes across the street from Bob's house. Manny expected him home within the hour. Bob would enter the house through its side entrance in a narrow, poorly lit alleyway between his and a neighbor's house. That was where Manny would surprise him.

He waited patiently and was startled when someone grabbed his hair, yanked his head back from behind, slipped a wire noose around his neck and tightened it. In less than a minute he lost consciousness and in three minutes he was dead. A van drove up and two men loaded the body inside. The van drove to the waterfront and the corpse was put on board a fishing trawler. The vessel then headed out to sea where the body, in a weighted, heavy canvas bag was dropped overboard in a relatively deep area of the bay.

News of the successful elimination was transmitted to Alyssa Ross on her cellphone. The simple message was, "As requested." In her office, high above Sixth Avenue in mid-town Manhattan, Ross turned back to the data sheets she'd been reading when the call interrupted her.

CHAPTER SEVEN

Bob never knew how close to death he'd been. Eric slid back into his "friend of Bob" mode and didn't tell Bob about the preemptive murder across the street from his house. In actual fact, he and Bob had communicated little in the past few months after Eric had called with news about the discovery of Chris's body.

Back in Yonkers, Oscar Gleason wondered why he hadn't heard from Manny about his assignment. Had it come off as anticipated or had there been an unanticipated hitch? It was very unlike Manny to go silent at a time like this. Oscar had to conclude that their scheme to eliminate Hillman had not worked out as expected. A simple phone call to Hillman's office confirmed that their target was alive and well. Oscar was left to wonder.

Alyssa Ross, in contrast, was given a full report and was pleased to learn that her assignment to Eric had been handled competently with the expected outcome. She was left to wonder if this would be enough to calm down the situation in Yonkers. Was Oscar Gleason a problem? She thought not. Larry Crandall's wise course was to maintain his low profile, so he was not likely to stir the pot. That left Bob Hillman. He was an enigma. She would have to meet with him and discuss his desire for revenge.

All in all, the current landscape seemed to be coming under control.

She sent Eric two first class air tickets to Nice with an invitation to take his friend and stay at the Ross villa in Saint-Tropez. She liked to reward good performance.

CHAPTER EIGHT

Alyssa Ross was most relaxed when she drove her car up the Hudson Valley to a restaurant near Hyde Park that offered the best Szechuan Chinese food she'd had anywhere.

She made the two-hour drive about two times a month and usually arrived alone. This was her retreat from the tension in her life.

She could feel Manhattan retreating into the distance behind her as she drove her Mercedes up the Taconic Parkway, singing along with the score from *Kiss Me, Kate*.

The restaurant was small, seating no more than forty patrons. At this hour, slightly before noon, only eight other diners were seated. One was a man seated alone and facing her. He occupied the table ahead of hers along the wall with windows facing the river. She'd never seen him here before.

He was dressed in grey corduroy slacks with a quarter zip sweater over a blue dress shirt. She guessed him to be in his mid-forties. He had the rugged good looks of a man who spent time in the out-of-doors.

He saw a woman about his age dressed casually in a hounds-tooth woolen skirt and rust colored cashmere sweater. Her streaked blond hair was pageboy style with bangs. He didn't think her especially attractive, but rather serious-looking. Her outfit could have fit in any decade from the fifties on. Martha Stewart was whom she brought to mind. She wore a gold band on her left hand.

They looked at each other, wondering what the other was thinking. Today she was feeling bold and uninhibited. She was curious about this guy and what he was about.

There was nothing to lose so she made a move, speaking to the stranger without seeming the coquette.

"Hello, stranger. I've not seen you here before, and I come here often. Is this your first visit to Sally Chu's?"

"Yes it is, stranger. My home is San Francisco and I miss its Chinatown with its superb Chinese food. This restaurant was recommended by a friend back home, so here I am. I assume you live in this general area since you come here often."

"Yes, I live in Manhattan. I don't think you'll be disappointed in the food here. The food and the ambiance are hard to beat."

Bob welcomed the conversation. He made an effort to sustain the contact. "Now that we've broken the ice why don't we sit at the same table? Could be yours, could be mine. We can keep the empty table as a fallback position, if that becomes advisable."

Alyssa was responsive to the invitation. "Okay, stranger, I'm going to join you at your table."

With that Alyssa made the move and introduced herself as Gabriela. He, in turn, used a false identity. Last names were withheld by unspoken agreement.

271

"So, Gary, you said you're from San Francisco. Tell me what you do."

"That's simple. I run an energy company out west. How about you, Gabby? You told me you're living in Manhattan."

"I run a transportation company, mainly overseas cargo transportation."

"That's interesting since as an energy guy I'm quite interested in transportation. That sector is one the largest polluters of our atmosphere and I'm quite involved in trying to get polluters to convert from less dependence on fossil fuels to more acceptable renewals. Now that you heard my pitch, do you want to move back to your table? Or can we drop this serious business talk and move onto more trivial matters?'

"I'd like that, Gary, but I am interested in your ideas on saving energy and polluting less. Maybe we'll come back to that."

Small talk continued through a terrific meal with more drinks.

"That was really fine Chinese food. I know what brings you back here, Gabby."

Time was running out for her if she was going to get back to New York by seven. Maybe that was what pushed her to make a brazen suggestion.

"Gary, why don't we take a room for the afternoon and bring a nice bottle of wine with us? I'd like to continue this conversation in a more private setting."

Bob hesitated. The invitation was clear and would be a very pleasant way to wind up this highly satisfying excursion.

"I wish I could take you up on what sounds like a delightful way to spend the remainder of the afternoon, Gabby. I'm afraid my loyalty to a woman, whom I've just begun to see in a serious way, makes me reluctant. I really am sorry."

When she looked back, Alyssa could only wonder how she'd surrendered her better judgment and extended an invitation to commit adultery.

The New York mayor's annual spring bash was a very successful affair. It raised a huge amount of money for the fall campaign. It also brought together a large number of highly influential people in a friendly setting.

Bob Hillman was there at the invitation of his friend George O'Reilly. He and George were chatting with Victor Brandt, the husband of one of the mayor's major supporters. They were deep into the president's failure to latch onto global warming and develop a policy embracing alternative energy sources.

Brandt stopped and turned to the voices behind him.

"I want you two to meet my wife, Alyssa." He gently turned one of the women in the threesome behind him and ushered her forward.

"Alyssa, I want you to meet Bob Hillman and George O'Reilly."

Alyssa stepped forward to shake hands with the two men with her husband. She was speechless for a moment, doing a double take. Bob quickly stepped in and rescued her. "It's a pleasure to meet you, Alyssa. I'm Bob and this is George."

Alyssa quickly recovered her composure. "I'm very pleased to meet you both. How are you two connected to the mayor and his campaign? I assume you're Democrats. Are you both New Yorkers?"

Bob continued as the spokesman. "George works for the mayor. He and I are old friends. I guess that's how the net extends and hauls in more donors."

Brandt was quick to add, "Alyssa is not a camp follower, fellows. She manages a very large transport company and is one of the mayor's major donors. If anything, I'm the camp follower," was Victor's way of more fully introducing his wife.

Bob was feeling playful with Alyssa. "Maybe you'd be so kind as to show me to the bar, Alyssa. George and I haven't had anything to drink yet. I had an exhausting day and could use some liquid intake."

"I'd be only too happy to, Bob. Just come along with me. I think I can quench your thirst." She took his arm and they threaded their way through the crowded room. "Isn't this a laugh, Gabby?" She squeezed his arm.

CHAPTER NINE

Marjorie Cameron arrived a little early at her office hoping to catch up on some unfinished business. To her surprise two people were camped out on her doorstep. They introduced themselves as Ethan and Andrea Tyler, the husband informing her that he was a Sampson employee. She unlocked her office door and invited the couple inside.

"Would you like some coffee? It'll only take a few minutes and I'm going to make some for myself anyway," was her way of a friendly introduction. "I'm Marjorie Cameron, the Human Resources officer at Sampson. I guess you probably know who I am since you came to my office. Why don't you tell me what you're here to see me about?"

Marjorie had quickly sized up the couple. Andrea, the wife, was a pleasant looking woman in her fifties. She was conservatively dressed in a skirt and blouse with a long cardigan cable sweater. Her husband,

Ethan, was handicapped by a very unsteady gait and needed to use a cane to get around. He was thin and looked older than his fifty odd years. His clothes hung on him in a way suggesting he had been heftier when they were bought. His expression showed a mixture of anxiety and sadness. Marge felt a wave of sympathy roll over her before she heard a word about the problem they were bringing to her.

"Ethan is quite disabled, as you can see," offered Andrea. "We have good reason to believe his problem is work related and are hoping you can help us get some compensation from Sampson. Ethan has worked here for nearly twenty years and has an unblemished record. He deserves some generosity from his employer. His condition has worsened recently and there may be more disabling changes yet to come."

"Mrs. Tyler, you can be sure I'll work with you out of this office. First, though, I need some information. I won't slow us down with the basic questions that can easily be answered by perusing his employee record. What I need from you is an understanding of why you believe Ethan's handicap is work related. Let's start with that."

"I can handle that question, Andrea. It's pretty simple. Up until about a year ago I was as sure-footed as a circus tightrope walker. I had no problem with walking and standing. I did my work assignment as well as any man. Then I developed a problem in my feet. At first it was just a numbness, and that progressed to the point where my footing was uncertain and eventually forced me into a sedentary position instead of the more active line worker job I'd held for nearly twenty years.

"When I learned another member of our team had a similar problem, I became suspicious that something on the job could have something to do with it. I told this to a young woman who came to interview me about work at Sampson. I told her about the other guy with the same problem. Jim Healy. He was seeing a doctor at Columbia and Jim's wife gave us her name. I remember it clear as day because when Andrea told her the name, the woman froze for a minute."

"Ethan, you said your wife gave this woman the doctor's name. A woman doctor. What was her name?"

"Christine Dinsmore. Doctor Christine Dinsmore. When we tried to make an appointment with her we were told she was unavailable and they had no idea when she'd return to the clinic. That seemed odd but we just made an appointment with another doctor."

"What did the new doctor say was wrong with your feet?"

"He said it was a problem with the nerves. He called it a neuropathy and wasn't optimistic about a cure. He couldn't say if it would progress or just stay the way it was. He didn't offer any hope of it going away and didn't offer any treatment."

"Look, I'm going to discuss your situation with the president of the company and see how he wants to proceed. I can't believe he won't be sympathetic, much as I am. We have insurance for these kinds of work-related issues."

"Thank you, Ms. Cameron. Ethan and I will look forward to hearing from you," Andrea said. With that the Tylers left the office.

Marge tried to gather her thoughts. Eric told her his wife disappeared, but didn't say she was a neurologist at Columbia who was seeing a Sampson employee and was about to get a second referral for a very similar problem. Surely the woman who interviewed the Tylers was Denise Crandall doing her project. She and Chris must have discussed the two similar cases and agreed on a plan of action. Denise would have reported the finding to Mitch and expected him to take some action. The logical next step would have been to bring in OSHA. That never happened. The next step turned out to be two murders. What was Mitch's role in this? She was now being drawn into this matter contrary to the initial disinclination she'd expressed to Eric.

CHAPTER TEN

With a lot on his mind, Larry packed up to go home and was about to lock up his office when Marge appeared in the doorway. She had her coat on and suggested they walk out together to their cars. Nothing unusual about that, but the expression on her face was anything but friendly.

He locked up and they walked silently out toward their cars.

"Larry, I need to talk to you about something that's been gnawing at me. Why don't we get into your car and I'll tell you what's on my mind."

This had an ominous ring to it, but he had no choice but to hear her out. He already had a lot on his mind and didn't welcome any additional headache material.

"Okay, Marge. Why don't you get in on the passenger side and I'll start up the car to get the heater going."

They both got into his car and he started the engine.

"Larry, I know about Mitch's role in the death of Denise. It's a pretty ugly story. I'm sure she reported to him about the toxic atmosphere in the plant and probably expected that he would contact OSHA to have it investigated and taken care of. He never did, and shortly after that Denise was dead and a neurologist disappeared. I think he fingered her to whoever did the killings in order to cover up the toxic problem. What I don't know is whether or not she passed the same information along to you. Or if Mitch did."

"I don't know where you're getting that information, Marge. I'd never do anything to hurt my daughter. Moreover, I never was given a heads-up by Denise about some 'toxic problem.' Someone is feeding you a line of misinformation for a reason I can't figure out. You're being used, Marge."

"Thanks for the warning, Larry." Marge was unsure how much of Larry's disclaimer to take at face value. She was willing to give him the benefit of a doubt. It was possible he never knew about the toxic environment before Denise's death.

"I'm getting out now, Larry, but before I go, I've set up a meeting for us both with Ethan Tyler and his wife in two days. He's a worker who's suffering from the effects of the toxic atmosphere he worked in for several months. I told them I'd take their case to Sampson and believed the company would have a sympathetic ear. Here's his folder. I suggest you read it and have a course of action staked out for these very desperate people when we meet with them. You may want to talk with our insurers to get the take on their responsibility. I'll tell your secretary when the meeting will take place. Goodbye, Larry."

CHAPTER ELEVEN

L eaves were blowing across the parking lot at Sampson on a chilly fall afternoon. Ethan and Andrea Tyler parked in one of the available visitor spaces. They were unsure what to expect, but Ethan was not optimistic.

"These guys don't part with money very easy. I think we'll get a lot of words and not a lot of cash. Maybe we would have been better off hiring a lawyer. Trouble is we can't afford one and they'd only take the case if they got a big piece of any money that was offered. We've been over this a dozen times and here we are, just the two of us, hoping we'll be lucky for once."

"Okay, Ethan. Zip up your jacket and let's see what they offer."

The couple walked in through the main door. Ethan was quite hobbled by his bad legs. He was using two canes, preferring that to a walker. They headed to Larry Crandall's office where his secretary then steered them into a small conference room with a table and six chairs. No one was in the room. They were offered coffee and both accepted.

After a short wait, Larry Crandall came in and introduced himself. He was carrying a folder and laid it on the table in front of him. Marge Cameron was last to arrive and gave the Tylers a friendly smile. She sat apart from Larry and the Tylers sat opposite them.

The atmosphere was a bit tense. Larry started out by summarizing the facts of Ethan's case. The facts were well known to all of them. He next expressed Sampson's sympathy for Ethan's plight. He then recounted their insurance company's stance, based on the same facts he had spelled out at the outset. The insurer had been unwilling to conclude that Sampson was to blame for Ethan's problem but was willing to make a one-time payment to match one offered by Sampson. It all came to a one-time payment of eighty thousand dollars and included the termination of Ethan's employment at Sampson.

The room was silent. Marge was stunned. The payment was less than a year's pay. Andrea Tyler began to cry. Larry had nothing else to say. The insurer didn't think the case was made that Ethan's problem was clearly work related. Unless that could be proven they didn't consider their client to be responsible.

The next few moments would always be remembered by Marge as if the scene was run in slow motion. On the contrary, the events happened very quickly. Ethan Tyler drew a gun from his jacket pocket. Larry dove toward Marge in an effort to get them both some sort of cover behind the table. Before he could pull her down to the floor he took two bullets in the chest, fell backward out of his chair, and never uttered a word. Ethan stood up unsteadily, looked down at Larry and, with a crooked smile on his face, put the gun under his chin and fired once into his head. He fell forward onto the table. Andrea Tyler never stopped screaming. It all happened before Marge could get up from the floor where she lay alongside a very dead Larry Crandall.

Two people were dead. Marge hugged Andrea and tried to get her to stop screaming. Larry's secretary called 911 and the police arrived in less than five minutes.

Andrea Tyler admitted her husband had been depressed but she never knew he had a gun. A note to her in his jacket pocket indicated that he anticipated this outcome unless a generous offer was made by the company. He wrote of his love for her and was sorry to leave her all alone. Without his legs he only saw himself as a burden.

For Marge it was a sad ending to her employment at Sampson. She had been planning to leave Sampson and set out on a new career path. She called Elaine and braced herself for the expression of anguish she would release. First Elaine's daughter and now her husband, each taken away violently. Even though she and Larry were separated and heading for divorce, their years together had left good memories.

CHAPTER TWELVE

Word got back to Oscar as well. He wasn't sure how the death of Larry would play out in terms of the Sampson-York relationship. Elaine Crandall now owned Sampson and Oscar had never even met her. He was unsure how to keep the same products flowing even if she was unaware of the relationship he'd had with Larry. The first step would be a friendly meeting where they could get to know each other. He'd know soon enough if she could be convinced to take an absentee ownership role and let him take over the management headaches. After all, she had no experience running a company. He made the call and arranged to meet Elaine in her office at Sampson.

Elaine wasn't sure how to handle her new role as president of Sampson Industries. It was far outside her range of skills and experience.

She finally settled on a call to Bob Hillman, a guy with experience running a large company.

Bob was more than willing to give advice to Elaine and arranged to meet with her several weeks hence. In the meantime, Elaine had her meeting with Oscar Gleason.

The York president was very congenial and offered his condolences for the loss of her husband. Since he and Larry had maintained a handshake relationship there were no documents for them to review. Moreover, he quickly determined that she knew nothing about the relationship between York and Sampson. Having a clean slate to work with, Oscar fed Elaine a very abridged version of his company's relationship with Sampson. It was a matter of record that York was Sampson's largest customer.

He told her that he wanted to continue their good business relationship. Elaine indicated that she saw no reason to change that. She admitted that she was a neophyte in the business world and had asked a good friend to help her decide what her role should be with the company. He would be counseling her shortly so she had to take a wait-and-see attitude about any future changes.

Oscar offered to help her with any management issues that might arise in the future while she waited to sort out her role. She thanked him and said she'd contact him if the need arose. With that, the meeting ended.

Through it all, Elaine maintained her composure. After he called to set up the appointment, she recalled an early evening when she returned home and found Bob Hillman talking with Larry in the study. They hadn't heard her come in so she was able to eavesdrop on their conversation.

Larry hadn't named Oscar Gleason as the actual murderer of her daughter but certainly left the impression that Gleason was York's top dog and likely the one to give orders of that nature. The likelihood of her welcoming any help from him in managing Sampson was zero. She'd discuss this matter with Bob.

As he drove away, Oscar felt somewhat reassured that the Sampson-York relationship would survive the death of Larry Crandall. The only fly in the ointment was the friend coming to advise Elaine on a future course. He kicked himself for not learning more about the advisor but didn't think a first meeting was the time to probe too deeply into Elaine's plans.

CHAPTER THIRTEEN

Springtime in New York was not unlike San Francisco. Bob had no complaint about the weather. He and Leslie were seeing each other almost every day and beginning to form the close attachment he had thought was only possible with Denise. His spirits were up.

The phone call from Alyssa was a surprise. They had kept their distance by mutual agreement. He had no idea why she wanted to meet him at her office. It sounded all business. He accepted her time and date.

Ross-Wagner had its headquarters in lower Manhattan on the top two floors of a new thirty-story high-rise office building near Chelsea. Bob cabbed over, took an elevator to the thirtieth floor, and was ushered into a classy waiting room. The coffee was excellent and the Danish was fresh.

The secretary was buzzed and brought Bob into Alyssa's office. She was dressed in a perfectly fitted grey suit with a pale blue shirt. He thought she looked great and seemed to fit into this sleek steel and glass office setting as if it was made for her, which it probably was.

Meeting her was awkward in a humorous way. She regretted her offer of an adulterous adventure but was grateful he had declined it.

No regrets and no follow-up. No harm, no foul.

Now, the two business leaders were face to face.

"Nice to see you, Alyssa. I was surprised by your call and have been trying to imagine what could possibly have inspired it. I keep coming up blank so I guess you'll have to spill the beans and clue me in."

"This is awkward for me, Bob. I know I have you at a disadvantage so let me 'spill the beans' as you said and get us on a level playing field. I know a lot about your involvement in the Sampson-York matter and that's the background for this chat. I may have to be a bit opaque in discussing it."

Bob began to understand why he was there.

Alyssa continued, "First off, I have to tell you that Eric Dinsmore is my personal attorney and *I know* what he knows. I know he deceived you but was conflicted by his desire to help you and him seek revenge for your losses while he remained loyal to me. He passed information on to me once it was clear that York was creating dangerous waves. You don't know this, but Eric helped thwart an attempt on your life in San Francisco by Manny Rufalo. Eric is your friend. Never doubt that."

"Okay, Alyssa, I'm stunned to learn about Eric's involvement in this matter as other than a grieving widower. I guess I accepted him as he presented himself and never questioned where his loyalties lay. He did deceive me but I guess no harm was done. I can live with that."

She continued, "Now for the opaque part, Bob. I'm aware of York Chemical's role in the death of Denise Crandall. Leave it at that. There has been too much violence arising out of the Sampson-York arrangement. I want the violence to end now. What's important to me is tranquility. Most of the players are gone. Oscar Gleason remains and will be relocated shortly."

Alyssa paused to let her point sink in. Bob sat in silence. He'd been able to surmise Alyssa's role to some degree. She obviously was more than the owner of a cargo shipping company. He decided not to press her on her role in the drug business.

"He's responsible for the death of the Crandall woman and understandably is the logical target of your revenge, Bob. I'm asking you to put this whole messy affair behind you and move on without *you* extracting your pound of revenge from Oscar. I'm trying to assure you that your revenge will be exacted. I'll stop at this point and see if you can agree to this."

"That's a lot to swallow, Alyssa. But I was already coming to the same conclusion without knowing as much about the matter as you do.

I'm tired of seeking revenge. I'm trying to move on and I think I have a companion to help me. So, my answer is yes. I hope Oscar Gleason pays a very high price for his self-serving destruction of two young, innocent lives."

"Rest assured, Bob. Oscar will feel the penalty for his actions. I've made sure of that. The decisions he made were strictly business ones. By the way, your reporter friend is doing a fine job sleuthing this case. I have one other request. Please don't use anything you learned here today to help her along."

Bob wasn't sure whether he was relieved. The darkness that had enveloped him for so long was beginning to lift, but he was unsure if it would ever be completely gone.

"You and I met under unusual circumstances, Bob, and were able to be very adult in the way we handled it. Now, we're having another unusual meeting. My hope is that you'll get on with your life and put the whole episode behind you."

"Alyssa, you'll have no problem with me. It's hard to imagine a violent matter like this coming to a peaceful conclusion, but that's probably the best way to end it."

With that he extended his hand. She brushed it aside and gave him a warm embrace instead.

CHAPTER FOURTEEN

The apartment was chilly on a brisk winter evening, but Bob and Leslie were more than comfortable under the heavy down quilt, even without any clothes. The takeout Korean wings and some very good Korean beer had only satisfied one of their hungers. The sex that followed had satisfied each other. They'd been apart for nearly two weeks and they each felt a need to make up for lost time.

Leslie sensed Bob was more at ease than usual. He'd made no mention of the Sampson affair. Leslie enjoyed him even more in his less tense mode. For her part, though, the Sampson affair was an unfinished story and that didn't allow her to match his relaxed state with one of her own.

Writing her next chapter in the bloody affair, she had a lot of ground to cover. The deaths of Sampson's two principals, Larry Crandall and Mitch Trent, along with the failure of the police to uncover any illicit drugs at Sampson greatly enriched her story's appeal. Yet, there didn't seem to be a way to tie it all up. And now Bob seemed to consider the whole affair closed and off his plate. So many deaths and no clear connection nailed down was not a satisfactory closure for her.

She decided not to revive the matter with him. Their relationship was moving into high gear and this was not the time to rock the boat. She'd write up what she had and try to get into the same untroubled mode he seemed to be in. Later, much later, she'd find a graceful way to pull him back into the story and find out how he'd been able to drop it after he'd made such a big investment in uncovering the people who were responsible for the death of Denise Crandall.

Much later came a lot sooner than Leslie had imagined. She and Bob were having dinner with Eric Dinsmore and Marjorie Cameron at a popular rib house in lower Manhattan. It didn't take long for Sampson to get into the conversation. Each one of the foursome had a stake in that affair.

"I hear Elaine is hanging on to the reins at Sampson and beginning to learn the ropes," was Marjorie's way of introducing the topic. "I may be out of there but I'm still a good friend of Elaine's."

Bob cautiously ventured into the topic. "She asked me for some help, and I agreed to serve as her informal advisor whenever the need arose. Nothing more exciting than that. I think she'll do just fine as she assumes more and more control of the company."

"I hear Oscar Gleason made some overture to help out but she decided that Bob would be a better choice," replied Eric.

"Forgive me guys, but who is Oscar Gleason?" asked Leslie.

Marge jumped in here. "He's the president at York Chemical, Leslie, Sampson's biggest customer."

"Well, it makes sense that he might offer to help, although even I can smell a conflict of interest here," was Leslie's response.

"Wouldn't have mattered anyway, Leslie, because Gleason is leaving York. He's history," was Eric's contribution.

Bob was frowning. "I guess you should know, Eric."

Leslie had been listening intently and now saw some tension between the two men. "What do you mean, Bob?"

Bob realized that he had inadvertently opened a door that he was supposed to keep closed. Leslie was quick to pick up on it. Ever the inquiring reporter. He tried to close the door and protect Eric's insider role.

"Why don't we can this topic and move on to something else, like what's a good winter vacation spot for a novice skiing couple like me and Leslie?"

Leslie knew she'd gotten all she could out of Bob's slipup. Eric apparently knew more than he let on and Bob felt obligated to protect him. She'd get that sorted out, eventually. She was sure it tied back to the Sampson matter and that was her story to tell. Her instinct said Eric was the one she had to know more about.

CHAPTER FIFTEEN

What was the best way to decipher Eric? Leslie knew a lot of the Sampson tale but she was sure Bob and Eric knew more. That gnawed at her. To write a major crime story and know that some crucial information was missing was too painful to contemplate. She'd let the story rest while she searched for the missing pieces.

Marjorie was the first person she contacted and Marge had little to add that Leslie didn't already know. Eric was a lawyer with a small practice, the nature of which didn't seem to interest Marge. As a matter of fact she seemed surprisingly uninformed about his work, considering her own educational background and the closeness that seemed to be developing between them. Leslie knew a dry well when she encountered one. In the reporting game you had to sense when there was no more to be gained by further questioning.

Her attempt to bring Eric out was similarly unrewarding. She tried to arrange a lunchtime meeting, but his secretary was evasive and unable to set up an appointment.

After trying to learn more about his professional life on the internet she had come up with nothing new. She was becoming more convinced, not less, that there was more to be uncovered.

Finally, she realized that she would have to push Bob to divulge what he knew about Eric that neither Marge nor Eric himself had been willing or able to pass on to her. Sure, she was being intrusive, but that was just a crude way to describe a reporter's instinct to dig deeper than the obvious superficial layer. Tonight she'd gently probe Bob and hope she wasn't crossing into sensitive territory she hadn't been invited into.

CHAPTER SIXTEEN

With Larry Crandall now replaced by his novice wife as president of Sampson, Oscar Gleason was feeling confident that the gods were smiling down on him. The arrangement he and Larry had worked out would survive. He would eventually assume a serious role at Sampson, even if the wife wasn't sure yet about how far she would allow him to penetrate the Sampson boardroom. Time was on his side and he could be very patient.

Given that promising outlook, he was surprised to find two strangers waiting for him just outside his office as he prepared to leave. He didn't like the feeling that came over him.

One of the men, a non-descript sad-looking, thin, Mediterranean type spoke in a soft monotone. "You're to come with us, Mr. Gleason. The boss wants a few words with you."

Oscar could see he had no choice. He remained surprisingly calm. This could be just what the sad-looking guy said or a more ominous trip. He suspected the latter but wasn't going to wet his pants in anticipation. They walked out to a waiting car and Oscar sat in the back seat sandwiched between his two visitors. They drove off. Oscar Gleason was never seen again.

Alyssa Ross received a phone call that indicated her directions had been carried out. She hung up.

Her meeting with Bob Hillman and his agreement to call off his search for vengeance had been a necessary first step. She wanted peace and Bob agreed to that. She had told him Gleason was going away and that there would be a sufficient penalty. She didn't tell him that she wanted to sanction Oscar in a manner that would make no waves. If he, Bob, had done the job, it would most likely have resulted in a police investigation and that was what she wished to avoid. For her this achieved the peace she wanted. Peace was good for business. The alternative would have been to eliminate Bob Hillman. That would have been a far more complicated approach. It would have ignited the concern of his reporter friend.

Eric was aware of the act Alyssa had ordered but had no hand in it. As with many other such actions he was simply a loyal bystander.

CHAPTER SEVENTEEN

Leaving the concert at Lincoln Center, Bob and Leslie headed east to Shun Lee for some late night dim sum. Leslie was a bit distracted as she anticipated Bob's evasive response to her invasion of his relationship with Eric. She was determined to press him for information she was sure he was keeping to himself.

Once they were settled in their seats and drinks were ordered, she cautiously started her questioning.

"Bob, I have to get something off my chest. Please bear with me."

Leslie paused and lightly bit her lower lip. She was unsure where she was heading.

She continued, "We were pursuing our investigation of the Sampson affair, trading information and acting reasonably in concert. Then you abruptly and unilaterally chose to back off and drop the matter. You gave me no explanation; I think you owe me one. Then last night in

295

the restaurant you implied Eric knew something significant about this Oscar Gleason fellow that I was totally in the dark about, even though I was working on the Sampson matter much as you had been. That's my piece, Bob. I'll stop here."

Bob was silent and stared at his wine glass. He knew Leslie wouldn't back off. She was relentless and apparently had gotten a scent that she had to follow. His concern was how to avoid exposing Eric and Alyssa, thereby putting Leslie in danger.

"This is tricky, Leslie, so please bear with me. Eric is deeply involved in this whole Sampson affair. The death of his wife drew me to him as a fellow mourner looking for answers. While we worked together on the murders of Denise and Christine he was simultaneously obligated to forces involved at a much higher level. Forgive me for being a bit opaque here. Full disclosure to a *Times* reporter would be dangerous for you and me. You have to trust me. I backed off the case because I was asked to by a high-level person and because, frankly, I was tired of pursuing vengeance. I thought we could just melt away and resume our normal lives. I naively underestimated how committed you were to the story. My slip about Eric in the restaurant would have slid by anyone else."

Leslie now knew that there was another person involved in the case and Eric Dinsmore was close to that person. Bob implied that it was dangerous to present a threat of any kind to that person. He was warning her off. She also now knew that Oscar Gleason was a serious person of interest for her but he was either gone or soon to leave town. Bob was well-intentioned, but his ominous warning had only served to stoke her fires. Maybe *he* could melt away, but she was unable to, not with such a big piece of the puzzle staring her in the face. He'd called her a dogged journalist and that was a driver even stronger than he realized.

"Thank you, Bob. I know I was testing your friendship with Eric and promises you may have made to some mysterious person or persons. Now I'm going to test you some more and test myself as well. I *have to* pursue the leads you gave me. It's in my DNA. I know you want me to walk away the way you did, but for me that's contrary to my reporter's ethos."

Leslie took a deep breath and continued. "My suggestion is that we take a brief pause in our relationship so we don't keep pressure on one another. I'll pursue the case as I feel I must and will try to do it in a way that minimizes the danger. You'll have to trust me and know that I want to return to you in one piece and resume our relationship where we left off."

Bob took his time responding. "I'm not sure I can buy into your proposal, Leslie. I'll have to sleep on it. I don't want our love to be in competition with your career. That's hard for me to take. You seem better able to abide by that, but of course it's your career. On my side I only have my feelings for you. You have me at a disadvantage."

Leslie had hoped, unrealistically perhaps, that Bob would go along with what she was proposing; a very brief holiday from each other. She didn't think it would be so hurtful that he'd withdraw from her. He was more sensitive to any change in their relationship than she realized. The loss of Denise had affected him more deeply than even he appreciated.

Leslie felt that it was too late to retreat from her proposal. She'd have to accept his response as a temporary setback in their relationship and assume they would patch it up as soon as she satisfied her search for new information. Once again, she saw a serious romance beginning to dissolve before her eyes. Her career seemed to be a stumbling block that she didn't know how to set aside. The realization was demoralizing.

They finished the evening with very little to say to one another. The damage was done.

CHAPTER EIGHTEEN

Leslie visited York Chemical and asked to see Oscar Gleason. The receptionist was pleasant and informed her that Mr. Gleason was not available. When Leslie sought an appointment on another day she was told Mr. Gleason wasn't taking appointments at this time and she didn't know when he'd resume his doing so. Pressed a bit harder, the receptionist admitted that Mr. Gleason was not in touch with his office and she had no way to reach him.

Leslie was taken aback. There were ominous overtones here. Gleason's connection with the Sampson matter was hard to set aside and loss of life was no stranger to those involved. She thanked the receptionist, left her card, and went out into the street. Bob's concern about danger seemed to be better grounded than she had appreciated.

The only person left for her to talk to was Eric. Well, maybe the next to last person. There was the mysterious "higher up" person whose identity was being withheld by Bob. Leslie felt uneasy. Killing came too easy in this affair. Bob was trying, best as he could, to steer her away from such a fate.

Her call to Eric's office went through a secretary who promptly put it through to Eric when Leslie mentioned Bob Hillman's name.

"Hello, Leslie. This is a surprise. How can I help you?"

"Eric, what I want to talk to you about would best be discussed in person, either in your office or a convenient bar. Can you meet me this afternoon?"

"Sure, Leslie. Meet me at Kavanaugh's on Third Avenue near 28th Street in an hour. The place should be quiet by then and be an easy place for conversation."

They arrived almost simultaneously and, after a friendly hug, found their way to a booth in the back of the narrow but deep bar room. The place was almost deserted at this midafternoon hour.

"Okay, Leslie, you set up this meeting. I'll try to help any way I can."

"Thanks for taking the time to meet with me, Eric. As you know, I've been closely covering the Sampson affair for *The Times*. It's been a very twisted road to follow. I'm nearing the end of that road but it's recently taken a few turns that I think you can help me with. First, Bob has abruptly decided to end his quest to find Denise's killer and, of course, Christine's. This puzzles me. He told me he'd been asked to back off by a person best described as 'high level.' He didn't divulge that person's identity but implied that there was danger involved if a reporter became too curious. That's number one. Who is this person and how is he or she involved in the Sampson matter?"

Leslie stopped for a moment, straightened up in her seat, and continued. Eric offered no comment.

"Second, I first learned about Oscar Gleason in the restaurant a few nights ago when Bob inadvertently mentioned that you knew about Gleason leaving York. I tried to see Gleason but he's nowhere to be found. That's it. My crude surmise, based on these opaque pieces of information, suggests to me that someone told Bob to drop his search and that Gleason would be taken care of by them. That assurance may have been what bought Bob's willingness to stand down.

"Then I find Gleason is gone and I suspect he's followed the path taken by Christine many months ago. Whoever warned off Bob is probably the person who dispatched Gleason. What role Gleason played in the Sampson affair is only known, I suspect, to whoever gave the order to make him disappear. At our recent dinner it was suggested that you might know about this mystery and possibly about the person who told Bob to back off. The more I turn this over in my mind the more I come back to you as the answer man."

"Wow, Leslie, I can see how your mind works. I won't bullshit you. You'd probably see right through it. The person 'higher up' is not to be messed with. The identity of that person will not be revealed by me. Stay away from that person and I can tell you some things you want to know to complete your story."

"I get the message, Eric. I give you my reporter's word. When I say I won't disclose something, I mean it. In this case I don't even know the identity I won't disclose and I assure you, as a source, that I won't disclose your role in the matter. Please go on."

Eric swallowed hard before he began.

"Oscar Gleason was behind the killing of the two innocent women. They were blowing the whistle on some toxicity in the Sampson workplace. OSHA would come in and that would deal a damaging blow to the drug manufacturing scheme they were running.

"Other efforts out of York to keep the drug business secret were considered a liability by the large drug organization. Gleason was considered expendable and was eliminated. Bob's effort to find Denise's killer was also deemed a risk and he was asked to stand down in that effort. He agreed, having been assured that Gleason would pay a heavy price. I think he'd grown tired of his pursuit so it was easy for him to let it rest.

"I'm gonna stop here, Leslie. I think I've given you all you need for your story. It's all true. You won't be tripped up if you print any of it.

You have my word. I only ask that you keep me out of the tale and stay away from the organization."

"That's very helpful, Eric. I think I can write the story to a satisfying ending with what you've given me. Expanding it into a larger drug exposé would only lose sight of the well-circumscribed Sampson affair."

Leslie knew she was leaving parts of the story on the table. Following her instincts, however, she realized that it was time to wrap it up and move on. She was not self-destructive.

She needed time alone to think about her relationship with Bob. She let the cab drop her off several blocks from her apartment and went into her favorite neighborhood pub. The place was empty at this midafternoon hour, so she sat at the bar and stared at herself in the mirror. A glass of vodka on the rocks sat in front of her.

She'd underestimated Bob's concern for her safety if she pursued the story beyond the boundary of Sampson-York. That concern was an expression of his love. She'd pushed it aside and chose instead to forge ahead close to the very zone he'd warned her to stay away from. That hurt him.

When he'd chosen, without consulting her, to drop his pursuit of vengeance, he had assumed she would go along with him. Especially when he more than hinted at the prospect of serious danger. Her determination to go ahead took him by surprise. This brought them to a fork in the road and resulted in them taking divergent paths.

Leslie now realized that their relationship was paramount. She was a fool to think she could put it on hold and then simply pick it up when she was ready. No, she wasn't going to let their relationship die, even if she had to beg him to forgive her. This realization suddenly brightened her mood. She punched in his number on her phone.

ABOUT THE AUTHOR

A.S. Most is a retired cardiologist with a passion for mystery/thrillers. Harlan Corbin and Michael Connelly are among his favorite authors. Most's first book, No Loose Ends, is a thriller set in Washington, D.C. It follows a newspaper reporter and physician as they attempt to unravel the cover up of a V.I.P.'s medical illness. Most resides in Rhode Island with his artist/educator wife. He has two sons, one an attorney and the other a journalist. He is actively working on his third book.